THROUGH THE FIRE

TRADITIONAL REGENCY ROMANCE

ELIZABETH JOHNS

❀ Created with Vellum

To my sisters

PROLOGUE

"This is the first time we will be apart," Beaujolais announced sadly to her triplet sisters, who were sitting on the large canopied bed with her in their London townhouse. They were enjoying their nightly ritual of gathering in Margaux's room. Anjou, Beaujolais, and Margaux were the identical beautiful daughters of the Marquess Ashbury and his French Marchioness.

"It is not forever, dear," Margaux said soothingly as she brushed her sister's long ebony locks to a silky sheen. "We will be together again. There will be house parties, and holidays..."

"It was bound to happen sooner or later. I thought we would all be married by now. Yet, here we are, on the shelf!" Beaujolais exclaimed.

"I am happy to be claiming my space on the shelf if it means leaving the Marriage Mart! You must admit I have lost the ability to hold my tongue. It is best I leave before I ruin you all," Margaux said laughingly.

"Yes, dear, we know. But a convent? Did you truly think *Maman* would allow it?" Anjou asked sceptically as she flashed her brilliant blue eyes at her sister.

"No. At least they are allowing me to go to help with the

orphanage in Scotland," Margaux replied, apparently satisfied with her lot.

"I would wager *Maman* will have you back here in less than three months," Anjou taunted while she mindlessly twisted her hair about her finger.

"I accept," Margaux held out her hand to shake on it, never one to shun sisterly competition.

"Stop, you two," Beaujolais said with disgust. "Could you not be happy here? Could you not beg *Maman* simply to let you stay at home?"

Margaux shook her head. "As if our *maman*, grandest hostess in the kingdom, would allow her single daughter to waste away at home. But even so, it would not be enough. I want freedom, dear. Can you try to understand?"

Beaujolais had tears well up in her eyes, causing the violet hue to deepen. "I'm sorry, Marg. I will try to be happy for you, but I cannot understand it."

Margaux sighed. "You are the one born to be a duchess, Jolie. I will leave brilliant marriages to the two of you."

"Do not tease me about being a duchess. Besides, there are only two unmarried dukes in the kingdom. One is ancient and the other a recluse."

"Afraid we will curse you?" Anjou joined in taunting with her other sister. Since they were small, it had long been a source of amusement to tease Beaujolais. She had pretended to be a duchess when they had played as children and acted the most like one. It had not helped that their mother had encouraged it.

"You *have* already turned down at least a baronet, a mister, two earls, and a marquess," Margaux pointed out helpfully.

"None of them could be taken seriously! And both of you have had as many offers as I," Beaujolais insisted in her own defence.

"*I* have not," Anjou boasted.

"And neither of us professes to be open to *mariage de convenance*," Margaux added.

"That is because you do not allow anyone to propose to you," Beaujolais retorted.

"I cannot consider anyone else," Anjou said, looking away.

Margaux took her hand to comfort her. "It has been years without word of Aidan, Anj. Do you not think it is time to forget him?" she asked kindly.

Anjou shook her head and allowed her tears to spill down her face. "I need to do something. I cannot wait much longer for father's enquiries." She stepped down from the bed and began to pace as she wiped her tears away. Her love, Aidan, had gone off to the American war and had not been heard from since the hostilities had ended.

"What do you propose to do?" Jolie asked with a frown.

"I want to go and look for him."

"Go and look for him?" both of her sisters said simultaneously in disbelief.

Anjou nodded. "Charles has agreed to help me." Their brother, Charles, and Aidan had been best friends.

"*Maman* and *Papa* will never agree to that."

"They have and they will," Anjou answered quietly without looking at her sisters. "As soon as father's enquiries are complete."

Beaujolais cried in earnest then. "It truly is the last time we will all be together!"

None of the sisters argued, but enveloped one another in a hug, wondering how life would change without the other parts of themselves.

CHAPTER 1

*G*avin looked at the letter in his hand in utter disbelief. His heart was tearing in two. His brother, wife, and children had been killed when their carriage had slipped down the side of a cliff.

"This canna be true." He shook his head and fought back tears.

"I am afraid it is, my lord."

"My lord? No. I doona wish for it. I'm a simple country doctor. I have a humble life and practice here."

"I am terribly sorry for your loss, my lord. But you are, in fact, the eleventh Baron Craig now, and thus have some rather large holdings that are your responsibility."

"This was not supposed to happen. Iain had three strapping young lads!"

The solicitor looked grave. "Perhaps, my lord, it would be best for you to return to Castle Craig and see for yourself."

The solicitor was met with a blank stare from a set of startling blue eyes; a look that was common to those who had been met with grievous news, but who had not yet assimilated the ensuing change in circumstances.

"Verra well. I will join you there as soon as I have made arrangements."

Gavin went through the motions of closing up his house and seeing his practice into the capable hands of his apprentice, a graduate of Lord Easton's school. Of late, Gavin had taken many trips into England to the school in Sussex and had toyed with joining it as an instructor on a full-time basis, but he had never been able to cut ties with Scotland. How would he practice medicine as Lord Craig? He would have to find a way, while at the same time doing his best to carry on with his brother's works in Parliament.

Gavin had seen more death than most, but he had not been prepared for the loss of his brother, or of Iain's wife and children. They had been the last family he'd had left. He had never before given a thought to running the large Castle Craig estate, and hoped desperately that his brother had appointed a trustworthy steward.

His carriage was loaded with immediate necessities. His servants would send the rest of his belongings with those of his staff who wished to join him at the new residence. He had one final stop before setting off to bury his brother and begin his new life.

The carriage pulled through the gates of Alberfoyle Priory, one of Lord Vernon's estates that served as an orphanage. He had become attached to a family of children there; the boy was attending medical school, but the two girls were still in residence. It would pain him to leave these children more than anything else. In fact, since he had no family of his own, perhaps they would consider allowing him to adopt them.

"Dr. Craig!" Maili Douglas came running when she saw him and greeted him with a hug. She was promptly lifted off her feet into his arms.

"Hello, my love. Where is your sister?"

"In the sewing class."

"Would you be so good as to retrieve her? I would like to speak to you both."

The little girl wrinkled her forehead in concern, but then nodded and skipped off to find her sister. She returned with Catriona, to whom he gave an identical welcome.

"Hello, lass. You have grown again!"

"Am I not supposed to grow?"

"Indeed you are. Only not too fast." Gavin choked up as he thought of his three nephews, who he would never see again, and who would never grow any older...

"Why are you sad, Dr. Craig?" Maili asked.

"I found out that my brother and his family have died."

"Like our mama and papa?" Catriona cocked her head up to look at him.

"Yes, lass. Just like that."

Catriona and Maili crawled into his lap to comfort him. "Are you all alone like us now?"

"I am, and that is part of what I wanted to speak to you about. I have to move away, and will not be able to see you as often."

"Please don't leave us!" the girls cried.

"I was hoping you would come with me—and Seamus, too, when he is home from school. Would you like that?"

"Would you be our new papa?" Catriona asked.

"I would adopt you, yes. But I will never try to replace your papa or mama."

The girls threw their arms around his neck.

"That would be perfect."

"I will return for you after I have arranged everything with your guardian and buried my brother."

"Must you leave us?"

"I am afraid so, but I will be back for you soon." He exchanged hugs with the girls and took his leave to go and bury his brother and his family.

Gavin sat in the luxurious crested carriage he had brought back from his estate to retrieve the Douglas girls. It had taken several weeks before he had secured the papers of guardianship from the Duke of Loring, who had taken the children on at the behest of his daughter, Beatrice. The children had become endeared of her during her brief time as their governess at Alberfoyle Priory when she had been sent there in disgrace. Gavin had fallen for Lady Beatrice during her stay in Scotland, while her betrothal to Lord Vernon had been broken.

Gavin shook his head. He had been devastated when Lady Beatrice had chosen Lord Vernon over him, but looking back, he tried to be thankful. Perhaps they would not have been a good match after all, so far apart in station as they had been at the time. He had mistaken her for a gentlewoman fallen on hard times—rather than the daughter of a duke—when she was humbly working as a servant, then as a governess. He had still fallen in love with her, and even now cared for her and wished her well. But everything did happen for a reason he frequently reminded himself. He did not dwell on his disappointment in love, but neither had he given his heart lightly. He vowed silently he would not make the same mistake again. Inheriting his brother's barony, however, was another matter. If ever there was a man who did not desire to be lord and everything it entailed, it was he.

He truly loved his life as a doctor. He loved his modest cottage, situated in a beautiful park overlooking the lowland peaks. His father had kept a more humble household, but Iain had had full stables and several vehicles, and Gavin was astonished to find how many changes had been made to the property. His brother had apparently found a way to make the old pile of stones profitable, but Gavin had not had the chance to delve into the estate books. He had spent most of his time sorting out the guardianship of the Douglas girls and seeing to the burial and fulfillment of his brother's will, then to having his practice taken over by his competent apprentice.

He did not wish to return to the castle. The castle that once felt like home had felt cold and empty, despite a household of servants. It had not felt right to be there without Iain, his wife, and their boisterous brood of boys. Gavin wondered if he would ever become accustomed to this unwelcome change in circumstance.

He reached Alberfoyle and gathered together the girls and a nurse who had agreed to stay on with them, and they began the journey to their new life. He hoped the castle would not feel so empty with the girls there.

Catriona sat in the corner of the carriage, quiet and tearful. Had he done the wrong thing?

"Have you changed your mind, lass? I doona want you to be unhappy."

"No, I have not changed my mind. I will miss my friends, but we will be closer to Seamus. I am thankful to have a home." She sat primly in the seat across from him with her hands folded, attempting to be brave.

"I am sad to leave my home, too," he said gently.

"I cannot wait," Maili exclaimed innocently. "We will be living in a castle, with balls and pretty dresses!" Her eyes were wide and her curls bounced enchantingly.

Gavin chuckled. Oh, to view the world as a child.

"I doona ken about that, lass. Perhaps when you are older." He reached out and tussled one of her curls affectionately.

Maili pouted adorably, and he had visions of her as a lovely maiden with scores of suitors. He dreaded that day. Catriona was already showing signs of maturity and he knew it would not be long before her time came. He realized the girls would need a governess to help with their education as ladies and made a mental note to advertise for one when they reached Castle Craig.

Maili bounced from window to window and seat to seat, practically climbing the walls of the carriage like a caged monkey Gavin had once seen. She was never quiet, always either singing or talking. She would certainly keep his hands full, he reflected. He had not noticed her enthusiasm before, but he had not been relegated to such a small space with her for long periods. Seamus and Catriona were much calmer children.

Out of nowhere, Maili climbed into his lap for a snuggle. Earlier, Catriona had fallen asleep against his shoulder. Perhaps they should stop for the night. When alone, he always rode on, eager to be home and not one for roadside inns. He needed to adjust his thinking now that he was a father. He would tell the coachman of the alteration to his plans when next they stopped for a change of horses.

As they pulled into an inn, a sleepy Maili looked up at him with her large grey eyes. "Papa Craig, when will we get a mama?"

He choked up at hearing her call him Papa. He looked over at Catriona, who was also looking at him expectantly, waiting for the answer to the question. His heart tightened in his chest.

"I doona ken, lass. I had not thought to take a wife."

Maili frowned and put her head back on his chest. Catriona looked away, disappointed. Gavin felt a tug at his heart, and hoped the girls would be happy enough with him. Once, several years ago, he had dreamt of having a wife and his own family. He loved children and had always wanted a houseful. He had fallen in love once, quickly and deeply, but when that relationship had failed, he had given up on love and marriage. It had been too painful to think about for a long time, but he finally felt he had reached contentment. It did not mean he wished to subject himself to it again. He would focus his love on these children.

The carriage gave a lurch as they stopped at the inn, and Maili unexpectedly proceeded to empty the contents of her stomach all over him. He sighed.

"Maili! I told you not to eat all of the comfits Mrs. Millbanks sent with you!" Catriona scolded.

Maili looked up sheepishly at Gavin. It was very hard to be angry at that face.

"I'm sorry, Papa Craig. I shan't do it again."

"Hopefully you have learned your lesson then. Let us stop for the night to eat, wash, and sleep."

After accompanying the girls to their room with their nurse and ordering a supper to be sent up to them, Gavin changed into fresh clothing and made his way to the parlour to find some dinner and have some time to himself. He would have to accustom himself to this new way of life as well. He was shown into the parlour, but was surprised to see a familiar face already seated.

"Lord Ashbury," he said as the Marquess stood to greet him.

"Lord Craig. It is nice to see you again." Ashbury held out his hand and shook Gavin's.

Gavin had made Lord Ashbury and his family's acquaintance when they had visited Alberfoyle Priory a few years earlier. Lord Vernon had been courting one of the Marquess's triplet daughters, Lady Margaux. She had been disappointed as well when Lord Vernon had married Lady Beatrice. But Margaux had likely married another by now.

"So you have heard, then?" Gavin asked with surprise at being called by his brother's title.

"I have. My condolences. Will you join me? My party has retired." Ashbury held out his hand towards the table. "You may not know I was acquainted with your father when I was a child. I spent much of my youth at a property near to Castle Craig, and recently I had become well acquainted with your brother. Lady Ashbury favours living in town, or France, so we are seldom in Scotland. I have opened a home for girls in the old dower house on the estate, and we come through from time to time. We are now here for a short visit, though I could happily spend the entire summer."

"Do you mean Breconrae? I vaguely remember the name Ashbury as the owner of the estate. I remember a dowager residing there when I was a child."

"Indeed. My mother. She has since passed on, but an aunt still lives there. Do you only now go to the castle?"

Gavin shook his head. "I have been back to Alberfoyle."

"Ah, yes, I imagine closing your practice and moving takes time to settle. Would you be able to join us for dinner next week? Lady Ashbury will be disappointed to know she missed you tonight, but will have my hide if I don't secure you for dinner. A quiet evening, I assure you."

"I would be honoured, thank you."

The Craig party was back on the road early the next day, eager to reach the castle while it was still daylight. The rolling hills and valleys were dotted with grazing sheep, and the lanes were narrow and steep. The girls held their breath several times as the carriage climbed, then descended quickly. For some time, the latter part of the journey was alongside the River Clyde, before they finally pulled through the massive iron gates of the Craig estate. This was the stage of the journey where Gavin had usually urged his horse forward with anticipation of greeting his family.

"Are we almost there, Papa Craig?" Maili asked for the hundredth time.

"Almost, lass. We are on the property now," he said with patience. "We will cross a large stone bridge when we are there."

"You own all of this?" Catriona asked, wide-eyed. Both girls were watching out of the windows with eager interest.

"Aye. Beyond the woods, the castle overlooks the loch, and the other side of the property is covered in fields of barley all the way to the village," he pointed and explained.

"Are there any other children near?" she asked hopefully.

"I doona ken, lass. I am certain there are some in the village."

They turned around the southern edge of the lake and a massive stone edifice broke into their view. Gavin had been raised here, but that seemed a lifetime ago. He had no desire to be the owner of a castle or bear the responsibility that went with it. The building looked as if it were from the age of Camelot. It appeared medieval, complete with turrets and archers' slits. He and Iain had captured their Guineveres here and slain innumerable dragons and Loch Ness monsters.

"I do not believe it. A real castle," Maili exclaimed.

"I told you it was, lass," he said with amusement.

"Is there a dungeon?" she asked, with frightening zeal.

"Of course there is. Don't be daft," her sister chided.

"Aye. And we lock up naughty children there," he said, chuckling and shaking his head.

Her eyes went wide, then narrow. "Are you bamming me, Papa Craig?"

"I hope you will never find out," he said with a wink.

Maili could barely contain her excitement as the carriage pulled to a stop. The servants had lined up dutifully to welcome the girls to their new home. Gavin held their hands and reminded them to mind their manners, then introduced them to the staff.

"Miss Catriona and Maili Douglas, this is Tallach, the butler, and Mrs. Ennis, the housekeeper. They ken more about the place than I do."

The girls made curtsies and the staff smiled. Neither Maili nor Catriona were used to the pomp of a house of this stature. Nor was he, any more. He had to suppress the disappointment he felt and smile too. He would make the best of the situation. He planned to do as much good as a landlord as he could as a doctor, once he learned how.

He watched fondly as Mrs. Ennis took the girls, who were hand in hand, through the great oak doors. Everything would be all right, he reassured himself.

CHAPTER 2

*L*ady Margaux Winslow had wanted to join a convent, but her parents had insisted she instead remove to their new orphanage for a short repairing lease. She had become enamoured with Scotland a few years before, when she had visited Lord Vernon's estate, to the north of Glasgow, while they were courting. Despite her less fortunate outcome, she still loved Scotland.

After Lord Vernon had married his true love instead, her family had attempted to divert her with trips to London, and to the Continent once Napoleon had been defeated. But she had come to the realization that she was content on her own. She had always been the most independent of her sisters, and decided that brilliant marriages could be left in their capable hands. She certainly preferred the spinster state to marrying for convenience. She found she was content helping with the orphans, though she did very little thanks to the competent staff which her family had appointed.

"What are you pondering, *ma chère?*" Margaux heard her mother ask.

"Very little, *Maman*," she remarked, as they sat darning socks for some of the children. Her parents had remained with her, hopeful to change her mind.

"We are having a guest for dinner tonight. Someone interested in contributing to the orphans."

"*Très bien,*" she said absent-mindedly. Guests were a normal occurrence with her parents.

"You should wear the emerald satin—bring some colour to your face, *non?*"

"If you wish, *Maman.*" Margaux cared little for what she wore these days.

"*Allons y.*" Lady Ashbury stood and directed her daughter to do the same. "I will see you at dinner."

Lady Margaux went through the motions of dressing. Her maid arranged her hair in a manner worthy of a ball, she noticed. She had to admit she had been experiencing a mild case of the dismals. Once she established a routine here she would come out of it, she was certain. She had never been one to sulk, but she needed to find something useful to occupy her time. No, she corrected her thoughts. To make a new life.

She made her way downstairs, determined to be more cheerful. If she could only convince her parents she was happy here, then they would be satisfied she was content.

"Ah, there she is now, Lord Craig," Lord Ashbury said as he saw her.

"Dr. Craig?" Margaux said, stunned as she met the eyes of the handsome doctor who had been enamoured of Lady Beatrice.

"He is now Lord Craig," her father corrected.

Whatever was he doing here?

"Doctor suits me fine," Lord Craig added as he bowed. "How are you, Lady Margaux?"

She dipped a curtsy. "I am well, thank you. I should offer my condolences then, I presume?"

"Thank you. It was verra unexpected. My brother had three sons," he said sombrely.

"I imagine it was much unexpected, then," Lady Ashbury sympathized.

"Hopefully your brother had a good steward. I met the old steward over a decade ago," Lord Ashbury remarked. "I imagine he has been replaced by now."

"He is the same, and has at least eighty years behind him." Gavin shook his head.

"Is he running everything to satisfaction?" Lord Ashbury looked doubtful.

"I have no idea if he is or not. I doona ken, other than to look at the repair of the tenants' cottages," Gavin said candidly with a laugh. "I was mad for medicine from an early age. I ken little about managing estates."

"*Mon Dieu*," Lady Ashbury sympathized. "Perhaps we may help."

"I am not sure anyone can help." Gavin shook his head in dismay.

Lady Ashbury took his arm and began leading him to the dining room. "Let us discuss this further over dinner. Everything looks better with good food, *non?*"

Lord Ashbury escorted his elderly aunt, Lady Ida, who also lived at Breconrae, and Lady Margaux followed quietly behind, wondering how having Lord Craig for a neighbour would affect her plans for a quiet life here. He was refreshingly different from the men she had run from London to avoid.

Gavin had not known Lady Margaux would be here when he had accepted Lord Ashbury's invitation. She was more stunning than he remembered, with her ebony hair, porcelain skin and light eyes. Yet, she seemed different somehow; more subdued than the outspoken young lady she had been a few years earlier, when he had met her at Alberfoyle Priory. That seemed a lifetime ago. He could claim no more than a slight acquaintance with her or her sisters when they had visited Alberfoyle. He had been completely overwhelmed with all three of the triplets before him at once.

No matter he had been raised the son of a Scottish laird, he was more uneasy in the presence of aristocracy now that he held a title. There would be different expectations. He knew he was being unfair to the Ashbury ladies. They had been nothing but kind. However, he could not help but feel inadequate around their beauty and sophistication. Subconsciously, he looked down at his plain black coat and pantaloons. He ought to see a tailor. Not that he wished to be a dandy, but he knew a man in his position must look respectable in a different way from a country doctor, who dressed more for practical reasons than fashion. He did not belong here.

"How long has it been, my lord?"

He looked up to see Lady Margaux's stunning blue-green eyes observing him questioningly. Lord Vernon had had a choice between her and Lady Beatrice. She was eyeing him expectantly. He should have been paying more attention. He had been lost in his thoughts.

"I beg your pardon. How long has what been?" he asked.

"How long since the accident," she replied with sorrow in her eyes.

"Three months," he answered, as he met her gaze.

"That is not long," Lady Margaux said quietly.

"No," he agreed sombrely.

"I imagine my nephew Easton and his wife were disappointed to lose you. They had great hopes of you joining them at their medical school," Lady Ashbury said.

"As did I. I have not ascertained how I will be able to continue practising medicine now."

"Perhaps you may help with the needs of the girls here from time to time," Lord Ashbury suggested.

"Aye. I would like that. Once I have everything situated. Thus far I have had my hands full learning to be a father," Gavin replied.

"I had not realized any children were left behind," Lady Ashbury said in confusion.

"No. These are my children," he said feeling mild amusement.

"Oh?"

"I took over guardianship of three orphans from Alberfoyle. They are the children of a gentleman. As I had become extremely fond of them, I decided I would adopt them. The son was serving an apprenticeship with me and is now in school in Glasgow," Gavin explained.

"Seamus?" Margaux asked with recognition.

"I thought they became Loring's wards?" Lord Ashbury spoke in a reflective tone.

"He has helped support them financially, but they chose to remain at Alberfoyle. I've supported Seamus through his medical studies," Gavin explained.

"And you have been there otherwise," Margaux remarked.

He nodded. "I saw them frequently when I was in Alberfoyle. I asked them to come when I found out I would be moving here. I hope I haven't made a mistake," he said sadly.

"A mistake?" Margaux questioned.

"I've no idea how to be a father. I think they are lonely. Seamus is away at school. It is just the girls and a nurse. I've advertised for a governess, but we have had only a few applicants thus far." He looked at a point on the wall above her head, lost in thought.

"Perhaps the girls would enjoy visiting here? It is not above three miles from your home," Lord Ashbury suggested.

"*Oui*. That is a wonderful idea," Lady Ashbury agreed. "It will give them a diversion, and us the chance to meet other girls."

"I would be happy to have them visit," Margaux smiled.

Gavin let out a sigh of relief.

"I am much obliged to you. I think they would like that very much." He smiled at them. "They are overwhelmed in the large empty castle. As am I."

"Everything is still new and different. All will be well in time," Margaux reassured him.

"Enough of me. How is your school?" Gavin asked Lord Ashbury.

"We opened ours not long after Vernon opened his. We take only girls who have fallen on hard times or been taken advantage of." Lord Ashbury spoke proudly.

"Who may not necessarily wish to join a convent." Lady Ashbury coughed and exchanged glances with her daughter.

Gavin felt perplexed but did not question.

There was no polite answer he could make to this, so he changed the subject.

"Where do you spend most of your time, then, if not at Breconrae?"

"I was here often before I married. My parents preferred living here. After I married, we spent many years in France before the war. My son appears to have little interest in settling down here, so we decided to convert the dower house to a home for the less fortunate. Aunt Ida lived here with my mother until she passed away," Lord Ashbury answered.

They all turned to look at Aunt Ida, who was chewing her food but staring into space.

"We split our time between our other homes," Lady Ashbury explained. "Usually we are in London at this time." She cast another pointed glance at Margaux.

"You need not stay here on my account." Margaux smiled mischievously at her mother.

Lady Ashbury stood, cutting the conversation off abruptly, signalling she and Margaux would move to the parlour.

"Lord Craig, would you mind if we skip the port and join the ladies?" Lord Ashbury asked, perhaps sensing he might need to intervene between his wife and daughter.

"Not at all. I am not much for port myself," Gavin conceded.

Margaux smiled to herself as she walked into the drawing room. Her father had not outright supported her decision to live alone, but he had not forbidden it, either. They settled themselves comfortably as they waited for tea to be brought in.

"How long do you plan to visit?" Lord Craig asked.

"That depends on Margaux," her mother responded.

Lord Craig wore a curious expression and glanced towards her with his piercing blue eyes. A lock of his dark hair had fallen over his forehead, and she had to turn away before she reached over to brush it back.

"I do not intend to leave." She looked at her parents with mild defiance. "I do not know how many ways to tell you, I am not going back to London."

Her mother sat quietly. She appeared to be controlling her temper.

"Dearest, I understand your sentiments, but perhaps after some time away you will reconsider," her father said gently.

Margaux shook her head. Her father sighed. Lord Craig shifted in his seat. He must wish himself anywhere but here at the moment.

Margaux had endured years of being paraded about before suitors, none of whom she had been interested in or felt a connection to. She and her sisters were frequently the focal point of gossip; three identical, exotic-looking French girls tended to have that effect. At first, she'd been pitied. Society had assumed she was wearing the willow for Lord Vernon. Then, fickle society had decided she was too fastidious in her notions and she had a sharp tongue. Some had even taken to calling the triplets Fire, Wind and Ice. Margaux was, of course, the fire-breathing dragon.

She had been terribly unhappy in London, never seeming to fit in, only being accepted for her name and her beauty. She had decided to give up on trying to find love. It was better to be alone than ridiculed.

"Please, *Maman*. Accept my choice. Go back to London to be with Jolie," she pleaded. Lady Beaujolais was one of her triplet sisters who actually enjoyed *ton* life.

Her mother shook her head and refused to look at her. She jumped to her feet.

"Would you excuse me?" Margaux asked. "I find myself in need of some fresh air."

"May I join you?" Gavin surprised her by asking, then looked to her father who nodded. They walked out to the terrace, where the sun was just beginning to set in the sky.

"I apologize, Lord Craig. My situation is hardly something you would wish to hear about." Margaux took a seat on one of the stone terrace benches looking out over the valley toward the Firth.

"There is nothing to apologize for," he reassured her. "I have spent the evening gauchely pouring out my problems to you." He leaned an elbow against the balustrade of the terrace. He was very masculine, standing there casually; so different from many of the starchy men Margaux had been courted by in London. She was aware of his masculinity, and it unnerved her as she felt his gaze on her.

"Not at all." She looked up and smiled at him.

"What troubles you then? Did something happen in London?"

He appeared concerned as he looked directly into her eyes. Suddenly, her problems seemed ridiculous. Why was she opening her heart to him? He was easy to talk to and that was disturbing. She guarded her next words as she stood and walked around, pulling petals off the flower she had plucked from the rhododendron.

"No one thing happened. But I am weary of the Marriage Mart. I want to make my home here, but my parents do not wish me to become a spinster, Lord Craig."

"I'm sure they only want what is best for you, lass," he said in a soothing voice.

"I am at peace with my decision, but they are not." She plucked another petal.

"I am sure in time…"

"They will not leave until I agree to return with them." The stem was devoid of petals, so she tossed it over the balustrade and returned to sit down.

"Will they not leave you for a time, perhaps?' he suggested.

She smiled. "I threatened to join a convent, so they brought me here, thinking I would change my mind. But I love Scotland."

He chuckled. "A convent?"

She nodded. No one took her seriously. "Why not?" she asked defensively.

"I suppose they think you may one day wish to be married."

"Working with the girls here will give me a worthy purpose," she pointed out in what she hoped was a reasonable tone.

"You might even wish to have children," he continued.

"Have you ever been to London, Lord Craig? To the *Season*?" She looked up into his eyes, willing him to understand.

"I've never been a part of that world," he answered.

"Fortunate man. I swore to myself I would only marry for love and not settle for a cold, meaningless arrangement. Love like my parents have is one of a kind. I want a partnership with mutual respect. It is a sad reality to be raised with such expectations."

"Although you and I have not had good experiences in love, it does not mean all will be bad," he reasoned softly, to himself as much as her, it seemed.

"Lord Craig, I am content alone. I do not understand why no one can accept my decision. My worth is not based on being married." She lifted her chin defiantly.

"Of course not, lass."

"Forgive me. I realize I am fortunate to have a choice in the matter. I sound like a petulant child." She sighed. "I should not be unburdening my problems to you. Thank you for listening." She curtsied and walked back into the house.

CHAPTER 3

*G*avin had not intended to confess his situation to his hosts, he reflected the next morning over breakfast. But there he had sat, at their elegant table, discussing the condition of his brother's estate, and how he had taken over guardianship of the Douglas children and brought them to live with him. He had been shocked by the turn of the conversation, and Lady Margaux's decision to retire to Lord Ashbury's Scottish estate. He would certainly welcome her help with the girls, but she seemed made for fashionable society. Would she truly be happy as a spinster, at a remote estate in Scotland? He shook his head. He knew little about ladies and their tastes. Perhaps she had suffered another disappointment after Lord Vernon. She seemed genuine in her desire to retire from London. Little about society appealed to him either. He had a wonderful relationship with Lord and Lady Easton, but he did not have to go about in society to do so. He knew they were not typical of the *tonnish* set.

His brother Iain had maintained a presence in London. He had been passionate about social reform and making laws to better conditions for the working poor. Gavin wanted to continue Iain's work, but he knew nothing about how to achieve that aim. If Lady Margaux stayed, perhaps she would not mind guiding him on social niceties in London.

He would not object to having Lady Margaux as a friend. She was intelligent and not afraid to speak her mind. She had certainly been frank with him last night, instead of batting her eyelashes at him as many females were wont to do. What was he thinking? They could not be friends, could they? He had to think differently now. As a doctor, he had been permitted unusual access to people's homes; glimpses of what happened behind those closed doors. All the rules were changed now, and not for the better.

He stood and walked toward the study, resolving to tackle the estate books today. He could no longer put it off. He probably needed to pension off old Wallace and hire a new estate manager, but first he needed to understand the condition and magnitude of what he was now responsible for. Lord Ashbury had offered to help. He would take Ashbury up on that offer once he had acquainted himself with his holdings and the situation they were in.

The scent of the study and old books swarmed his senses with nostalgia. He stood for a moment in fond remembrance of his child-hood here; and later, of engaging conversations with his father and brother. He dismissed his grief and walked forward to the desk—a desk that was piled high with unopened correspondence. He shook his head. His brother had never been organized, and apparently the steward's duties did not include sorting through the post. He sat before the massive oak desk and felt acutely out of place. He remem-bered his brother and father sitting here before him. How life had changed; almost in the blink of an eye.

"Papa Craig!"

Gavin heard his name echo through the house, followed by the pitter-patter of feet running down the stairs and through the hallway, before a sprite burst through into the room.

"Guid morning, Maili," Gavin said, fondly looking up at the young girl.

She climbed into his lap for a cuddle and kissed him on the cheek. Both girls seemed to need constant reassurance.

"Maili!" they heard Catriona call and subsequently she came running down the stairs searching for her sister. When Catriona reached the door, she pulled up at the sight of Maili sitting innocently in Gavin's arms.

"Catriona. I doona think ye should be running through the house, yelling at your sister," he chided softly.

"But...but..." her chin and bottom lip began to quiver and she burst into tears.

Oh, heavens above. He had no idea how to handle a crying female. He tried to correct her gently.

"What is the matter, Catriona?" he asked.

"M-M-Maili cut my doll's hair off!" She held up the toy, which had stubs of hair sticking up all over its head, as evidence.

"Is that true, Maili?"

He looked down at Maili, whose face instantly told him the answer.

"I thought she would look pretty with short hair," she replied naïvely.

"It was not your doll to decide!" Catriona wailed. "My mother gave her to me, and now she is ruined!" She ran away, crying.

Gavin could not blame her. He would not mind running away just now. He had to find a governess soon.

"Maili, go to your room until I decide what to do. You will have to apologize to your sister."

Hanging her head, the little girl slid from his lap. She looked at him with large tears in her eyes and then dramatically turned away to follow his command. He sighed loudly and put his head in his hands. Did all parents feel this incompetent?

He decided a visit to Breconrae would be a welcome diversion. If the girls could find something useful to do there and even make some friends, it would be a blessing.

There was a knock on the door, and his aged steward stood before him.

"Guid morning, Wallace."

"Guid morning, Lord Craig. I couldna help but overhear yer

situation."

"Yes, Wallace. We need to advertise more widely for a governess. Even in London, if necessary."

"Verra well. But what you need, m'lord, is a wife," Wallace answered bluntly.

"I beg your pardon?" Had he heard correctly?

"Ye need to adjust to your new life. Get married. Make babies. Find someone to help. I had just retired and not a week later poor Lord Iain had his accident," Wallace said sadly.

"You retired? Why dinna you tell me?" Gavin held out his hands.

"I couldna. But I'm too old to be here. It hurts to move. Takes me hours to move from my bed in the morning, m'lord."

"I see. And had Iain found someone to replace you?"

"I doona think so. I doona think he was looking so verra hard, though."

Gavin muttered a curse and ran his fingers through his hair.

"Ach, well, it canna be helped, I suppose. If you would be so kind as to go over everything with me, I will do my best until we can find a replacement. I will write to my friend, Lord Easton. He houses wounded soldiers until they are healed and ready to work."

Wallace shook his head. "I will assist you until you can find someone, but there are some things I canna do any more."

"I understand. I am grateful for anything you can do."

"I will advertise again for a governess. For now, I suggest you make the rounds to the tenants and become acquainted. They will inform your lordship of what needs to be done," Wallace suggested.

Gavin nodded. That sounded reasonable.

"Yer brother had a very large whisky operation, and began farming the crops to sustain it. Did you ken of it?" Wallace asked sceptically.

"I did. I doona suppose I understood it all. He mentioned he was fighting for legalization to distil it on a larger scale," Gavin said, with a feeling that he was about to be shocked again.

"Aye. He only distributed to a select few, and not publicly, although it was a dream of his. He oversaw all of the whisky-making himself," the steward said with a proud gleam in his eye.

"I doona wish to involve myself in something illegal," Gavin protested.

"I wouldna precisely phrase it as illegal. There will be some verra disappointed people if you were to cease the whisky operation, and a considerable number of workers would be unemployed should you wish to do so," Wallace said. His voice held a challenge. "Though there would be those who would be pleased to see it fail."

Gavin raised an eyebrow, but the steward did not elaborate. "I will look into it later. Continue."

"Then there is the matter of the solstice ball."

"Aye, it has been a tradition in my family as long as we have held the barony."

"And the mistress is the one who puts it together," Wallace reminded him.

"And I have no mistress," Gavin said, grimacing as the words left his mouth.

"Indeed." The old man nodded as if his pupil was finally mastering his lessons.

"That is only a few weeks away. Is there anything done?"

"Verra little. Perhaps you could enlist the aid of another lady this year," Wallace suggested.

Gavin looked dumbstruck.

"Wouldna the vicar's wife be a guid person to ask?"

Wallace scoffed. "Ach. I wouldna, but I doona fancy hell-fire and brimstone. Queer lot, the vicar and his wife, but ye must do as ye see fit." The old man shrugged.

"I need a governess for my new children, a new steward to run the estate, I need to greet the tenants, I need to learn how to farm and make whisky, and I have a ball to put on by the solstice. Anything else?" Gavin asked in disgust.

"A wife and an heir would not go amiss," Wallace reminded him.

"Of course," Gavin said, making no attempt to hide his sarcasm.

There was a knock on the door. Gavin looked up to see the familiar face of the housekeeper, who had been at the castle since he was a boy.

"Come in, Mrs. Ennis."

"M'lord." She gave a small curtsy.

Gavin twitched his neckcloth. This was all so uncomfortable.

"I need to go over menus and some household purchases with you, sir," she stated.

"Menus?" he asked with disbelief.

"Yes, m'lord. There is no mistress to perform the duties…" Her voice trailed off.

Not her, too.

"I am certain you are quite up to the task, Mrs. Ennis. You certainly ken more than I."

"No, m'lord. I couldna." She looked at him as if he had insulted her.

"You could. Please. For me." He pleaded. If he was given one more task he might snap.

She looked terrified, but must have seen something in his expression that made her nod and quietly leave the room.

"Wallace, how many other duties did the mistress perform?" he asked, though he did not really want to know.

"Lady Craig always saw to the household, the tenants, the children, the ball, the accounts…" Wallace ticked off the list on his rheumatic fingers as he spoke.

"Enough! Enough!" Gavin said feeling overwhelmed. "That will be all for today. If you wouldna mind seeing to the correspondence, I have someone I need to meet."

"Verra well, m'lord," Wallace said with a loud sigh.

Gavin sent word to the nurse to have the girls ready to leave in two hours.

He burst through the front doors and headed for the stables. He needed to think. He hoped a quick ride would settle him, for all he wished to do was travel to the ends of the earth and forget these last few months had ever happened. As he took the horse through its paces, including a fierce gallop that nearly stole his breath, he felt his anger begin to ease. He knew his temper to be ill-placed, but he was aggrieved. At Iain. At God. At the children. At himself, and at the wife he now needed but didn't want.

CHAPTER 4

*M*argaux decided that today she would dress the part her new life demanded. She knew it would anger her mother, but the more Lady Ashbury saw her in this role, the more she would become accustomed to the reality of it. Her mother was a force in society—holding extravagant parties and leading the *ton*. Donning a mob-cap to complement her plainest gown, Margaux wondered if perhaps she exaggerated the spinster costume for her mother's bene-fit. She had instructed her maid to pull her hair into a severe knot, and the crisp muslin and lace hid the lustrous waves entirely from view. She chuckled and thought the cap would have to go once her parents left. She might wish for a more simple life, but that did not mean she had no taste.

She wondered if Lord Craig would bring the Douglas girls to visit today, as she planned to make her way to the dower house to see how she could be useful.

She paused outside the door when she overheard her parents in the breakfast room. Did she dare walk in on them and start the argu-ment all over again? Or should she stay in the hallway with the picture of her grandfather staring at her?

"What have we done wrong, *ma chere*? Anjou is dashing about with

Charles, looking for Aidan, who is likely dead, and Margaux wishes to don her caps!" her mother said, exasperated.

Margaux guiltily reached up and pulled the mob-cap from her head. She should let them know she was there, but she could not make herself go further.

"It is a crime to waste her beauty," her mother said in a pitying tone.

"You do want her to be happy, no?" her father reasoned.

"*Bien sûr!* How could you ask such a thing?"

"She was not happy in society. Did you take no notice? Perhaps we should give her some time. Once she is away from everything she knows and has spent an interval alone here, she might change her mind. It is my belief she is not sure what she wants."

Thank God for her father, Margaux thought. She doubted she would change her mind, but she wanted more time without her mother's constant harping. Once they saw she was happy they would have to accept it.

"I understand what you are saying, *chérie*, but we cannot leave her alone here," her mother protested.

"Aunt Ida is here," her father pointed out.

Margaux could imagine her mother's expression at the moment. Aunt Ida was senile and pleasant, but would no better chaperone her than a puppy.

"*Oui*, she will make an excellent chaperone," her mother said sarcastically.

She heard her father laugh. "Margaux is old enough and has an excellent head on her shoulders. There is little harm to befall her here."

Her mother let out a sigh. "Perhaps we could return to London for Jolie's sake?"

"You believe Yardley or Summers will come up to scratch?"

The Duke of Yardley was horrid, in Margaux's opinion. She was not actually acquainted with him, but his reputation left her cold. He only wanted to acquire Jolie, not have a relationship with her. Summers was older than their father. But Jolie did not care. She had always wanted to be a duchess. Margaux hoped her father would intervene.

"He is paying marked attention to her, according to what Lady Easton writes." Lady Easton was the wife of Lady Ashbury's nephew, and was chaperoning one of Margaux's triplet sisters while Margaux and her parents were in Scotland.

"I wish I knew more about him. I think it would be wise for us to be there while they are courting," Lord Ashbury said. The concern in his voice was evident.

"Every part of me is hurting to leave Margaux here. I cannot feel easy. However, if we may return soon, I will go if you think it best," her mother responded. Margaux could hear the resignation.

"I do. She will be perfectly well. Perhaps the good doctor will catch her eye."

"She would be blind to not notice the beautiful, brawny Scot with his blue eyes and delicious burr." Lady Ashbury sighed in acquiescence. "Very well, *mon ami.*"

Lord Ashbury laughed. "I suppose he is handsome."

Margaux nearly choked. That propelled her forward into the room.

"*Bonjour, Maman.*" She kissed her cheek. "Good morning, Papa." She walked around the table to kiss his cheek before filling her plate.

"Margaux, your mother and I have decided to return to London for the remainder of the Season. We think it wise to be with Jolie."

Margaux turned and raised a questioning eyebrow, trying to look surprised.

"That does not mean we are giving up," her mother stated. "We are merely giving you some time to think. Though it will cause the tabbies' tongues to wag."

Margaux nodded. "I will be quite content here. The girls at the dower house will keep me busy."

"But what of your own children?" her mother asked tenderly.

"Not all of us are fortunate in love, *Maman.* I played that hand once and lost. I refuse to marry only to have children. Breconrae was good enough for *Grand-mère* and Aunt Ida to live in."

Her mother only shook her head in bewilderment.

"And Aunt Ida will be here with you for propriety," her father said to her with a conspiratorial wink.

"Thank you, *Maman* and Papa," she said. Her lips quivered as she endeavoured to keep a straight face.

Her mother stood. "I will go and direct the servants to pack. We should begin our journey as soon as possible."

After her mother had left, Margaux sat in comfortable conversation with her father. The butler entered and asked if she was at home to callers this morning.

"Who is here?" she asked.

"Lord Craig, and the Misses Douglas."

"Yes, of course. I was expecting them." Margaux rose to her feet. "Please show them into the parlour."

"Yes, my lady."

Her father followed to greet them.

"Good morning, Craig." He shook his hand jovially.

"Lady Margaux." Lord Craig offered a bow. "Do you remember Miss Catriona and Miss Maili Douglas?"

"Of course. Welcome." She curtsied to the girls.

"It is one of the princesses," Maili exclaimed as she rose from her deep curtsy.

"I am not a princess, Maili," Margaux said with a smile, thinking how she had purposefully tried to be plain today.

"You look like one." The child's admiration was undisguised.

Margaux laughed and took the girls' hands. "Would you like to meet some of our young ladies at the dower house? I am going there now."

The girls nodded with excitement and followed along with her in wonder.

～

"May I ask you to spare some of your time?" Gavin asked Lord Ashbury when Lady Margaux and the girls had left. "Yes, of course. I wished to speak with you also before we leave," Ashbury replied.

"Leave?" Gavin had not expected such a quick departure after last night's conversations.

"Let us remove to the study to discuss matters." Lord Ashbury held out his arm to direct Gavin across the hall, then closed the door behind them. He indicated for Gavin to sit down.

"We have decided to return to London, in order to become better acquainted with the gentleman courting one of our other daughters. I have convinced my wife to permit Margaux to remain here some little while. Perhaps Margaux will see reason once she is away from everything familiar. I am certain no harm will befall my daughter, but could I possibly ask you to keep an eye on her from time to time and send me word? I assume you will be bringing the girls here on occasion, and it would ease my mind to know how she is fairing."

"I would be happy to do so if Lady Margaux is agreeable to my visits," Gavin reassured him.

"Thank you, Craig. I have no doubt you and Margaux will deal well together. Can I offer you a drink? Scotland's finest." Before Gavin could respond to the cryptic remark, Lord Ashbury held out a tumbler of whisky that Gavin instantly recognized from its aroma as Craig. His brother might have capitalized upon the recipe, but it had been passed down through generations.

"So, are you one of the parties my brother has been supplying?" Gavin asked.

"Of course... along with half the aristocracy who are not fortunate to have our own still in Scotland. And those who envy his recipe."

"Half?" Gavin looked up with surprise.

"Craig whisky is found in the finest homes across Britain," Lord Ashbury said as he swirled the golden liquid around his tumbler and took an appreciative whiff.

"I had no idea," Gavin said completely in awe.

"It is, of course, not something to publicize until the legislation is passed. The taxation on the legal distillers makes wide distribution difficult for most to enjoy. You should consider taking your seat when you are more settled here and add your voice to the matter," Lord Ashbury advised.

Gavin nodded. "I had planned on it, but I am in over my head at the moment."

"Please tell me how I can help," the older man said kindly.

"I doona ken where to start. I am inadequate from my dress to my lack of wife. It now appears I must become a farmer, too. I have a ball to plan, my steward was pensioned off, and I need a governess. If you can advise me on any of it, I will be ever grateful."

"My goodness. I can certainly put in some enquiries as to stewards when we are in London. There are always second sons of gentry who would be just the thing. Lady Ashbury would be more helpful with your other dilemmas. Especially the wife."

Gavin tried not to choke. "I had thought Easton might have a veteran or two who might fit the bill."

"An excellent notion. I will consult with him as well," Lord Ashbury said as he rang the bell and asked for his wife. She came dashing into the room a few minutes later.

"Lord Craig, *excusez-moi*! I did not know you were here. How do you do today?" Lady Ashbury held her hands to her chest as she came into the room and saw him.

"Verra well, my lady." He had risen to his feet when she entered and offered a bow of greeting.

"Lord Craig requires our assistance. Would you be able to make enquiries with respect to a governess while in town?" Lord Ashbury explained.

"*Oui*. I would be delighted." She smiled at him.

Gavin thanked her, but still did not feel relieved.

"Is something else the matter? You look worried, *non?*"

"Nothing you can help with, unfortunately, madam. I must next approach the vicar's wife and see if she can assist with plans for the solstice celebration. It would seem it was another of the late Lady Craig's duties."

"I imagine there is a large void to fill with a house of such a size.

Not many ladies are prepared for running such a grand household. Have you considered taking a wife?"

Gavin raised his eyebrows, but did not answer. He did need a wife, but why was it so humiliating to admit it?

"I imagine if you were to ask Margaux for assistance, she would be delighted to assist with the girls. I give her one week to be bored beyond her senses. She believes she will help with the orphans, but even now we have more staff than we need."

"She has already offered to teach my girls," he said, as if he would be placing an imposition on Margaux and her time.

Lady Ashbury waved her hand. "She was always my organized child. She has been involved in the running of my household from a young age. She must keep herself busy or she becomes restless."

"But would it not be improper? She is not married," he questioned. He had no desire to ruin Lady Margaux by association.

"There can be no objection when she has her aunt to chaperone her."

Gavin thought of the aunt who had been present—yet not present —at dinner the night before. Was she the intended duenna? Gavin was grateful it was he and not some scandalous rake with whom they were entrusting their daughter's care.

"I will consider asking her, madam, if the vicar's wife is not amenable. I doona wish to impose on Lady Margaux."

"I imagine she can be a great deal of assistance to you until you find the people you need."

"Thank you, I will think on it. I wish you a safe journey. I promise to keep you informed, Ashbury. My lady." He kissed her offered hand and shook Lord Ashbury's.

Gavin turned to go seek out the girls and missed the wink and large grin that passed between Lord and Lady Ashbury.

Meanwhile, Margaux had been giving Catriona and Maili a tour of the home for abandoned young ladies. She began with finding the house-mother and introduced them.

"Mrs. Bailey, may I present our new neighbours, Miss Catriona and Miss Maili Douglas. They are now living at Castle Craig, and were previously at Alberfoyle."

Mrs. Bailey nodded understanding and gave a curtsy.

"Welcome to Breconrae, Miss Douglas and Miss Maili."

"Lord Craig has been unable to secure them a governess as yet, so we thought they might enjoy joining our lessons for now," Margaux explained to the house-mother.

"Verra well, milady. Why doona we introduce ye to the other young ladies and see what ye think?" Mrs. Bailey smiled at Catriona and Maili, then turned to lead them through the house.

The girls were shy on first inspection, but it did not take them long to feel comfortable in the house once they realized it was much like Alberfoyle. Catriona had grown into a friendly young lady, and Maili was by nature curious and talkative. Margaux watched the children settle, and studied the house for areas that might need improvement.

"Is there anything you need today, Mrs. Bailey?" Margaux asked curiously. Never had she been to an orphanage that did not need something.

"I canna think of a thing at the moment. Yer father has the place running without a hitch."

"No doubt. I would still like to be of use." There was no plan for her to be there; certainly not to work.

"If I think of anything I will surely let you ken," Mrs. Bailey said and left.

She was being dismissed. The house-mother likely assumed this was merely a passing fancy of hers and only told her what she thought she should. She would have to prove herself. The beauty of the orphanages Lord Easton had started was that the children were taught skills to be self-sufficient when they left. The orphanage was run more like a training school and the girls learned while helping. There was little for her to do, other than some small amounts of sewing—and even that was mostly done by the orphans.

She needed to find something with which to occupy herself, but she would not worry much yet. She was certain to find usefulness in one way or another in time. She would speak to the vicar's wife and visit the villagers. Perhaps they had not seen their needs attended to in some time; at least since her grandmother's passing, if Aunt Ida's current state was anything to go by.

She watched the Lord Craig's daughters. They seemed at ease in these surroundings, possibly more so than as wards of a lord in a large castle. However, they would be expected to be brought up as ladies and would need a different type of education from most of the girls at their school. She could work with Catriona and Maili until a governess was found for them. Maybe by then she would have found a worthy way to occupy her days.

After she considered the girls had spent enough time at the Dower House to feel comfortable and make some new friends, Margaux led them back to the main house. She could discuss her ideas with Lord Craig and see if he agreed.

"Pardon me, my lady," Mrs. Bailey stopped her on her way back to the house and pulled her aside from the girls. "Forgive my sayin' so, but I doona think it is a guid idea, milady, to teach them with our girls. They need to be learning more genteel things if they are to be educated as the daughters of a baron."

Mrs. Bailey had almost read her mind, but she did not like her tone.

"Such as dancing, music, languages, and art?" Margaux tried to keep the bitterness out of her voice. She had benefited little from such an education.

Mrs. Bailey nodded.

"I suppose you may be right. I will discuss this with Lord Craig. I had hoped it would be acceptable for a time."

"But ye put them here and they willna want to stop. It's best to start them as ye mean to keep them," the woman insisted.

"It is for Lord Craig to decide," Margaux said firmly.

"Verra well, milady." Mrs. Bailey curtsied and left briskly.

Wonderful. Margaux had managed to raise the house-mother's bristles when she desperately needed to find a place here. Of course, they would tolerate her no matter what, since her father owned the estate, but that was not the same as acceptance. Why did she always voice her opinion so freely? It had deterred many a man in London who had wanted her to be nothing more than a porcelain doll for them to display. Apparently it had been unacceptable for her to be beautiful and also be able to think.

She fell into step with the girls along the path.

"How would you like to learn some new things?" she asked them.

"What kind of new things?" Catriona asked warily.

"To play the pianoforte and sing, or to paint, or learn to speak French?" Margaux suggested.

"But I want to learn to dance," Maili protested.

"Of course. Dancing is an essential part of a young lady's education."

"Are you going to teach us?" Catriona asked suspiciously.

"If it is acceptable to Lord Craig," Margaux added.

Both girls threw excited hugs around her, and this was the scene upon which Lord Craig stumbled upon as they came up the path.

"Papa Craig!" Maili shouted with unsuppressed elation. "The Princess is going to teach us to dance."

"She is?" he asked, amusement warming his tone as he looked toward Margaux with his pleading eyes. There was something in that look she could not read.

"I shall be pleased to instruct them in ladylike accomplishments until you have found a governess, should you wish me to do so," Margaux offered.

"I would be eternally grateful for your help, my lady," he said quietly.

She nodded and their gazes locked. They walked in silence for a few moments.

"Lady Margaux, will you be attending the musical at Squire McDougal's?"

"I—" Margaux hesitated and frowned. "I had not thought of attending any social events here."

"It will be nothing like a London musicale, of course."

"I—" Still she hesitated.

"And your aunt, of course." His eyes held a mischievous gleam.

Their eyes met again and they both laughed.

"Very well. I would be delighted to make the acquaintance of the neighbours."

Gavin gathered the girls into the carriage. Maili was already attempting to practice her dance moves in the small conveyance. Catriona was lost in thought. Gavin dared to hope his situation might improve with the help of Lord Ashbury and his family.

"Papa Craig, why were some of the girls so big?" Maili held out her arms to indicate their bellies. "They look like Mrs. Millbanks did when she was going to have a baby."

Gavin had to take a deep breath. He had known this was coming, but still was not sure how to answer.

"They are going to have babies, Maili," he said, seeing no reason not to be truthful.

Maili's eyes grew wide. "But they are not married!" she protested.

"Nay, lass. You doona have to be married to have a baby."

"Papa Craig, where do babies come from?" she asked.

Naturally, that was the next logical question. He should have seen it coming as well. Perhaps jumping from the carriage would be less painful than answering.

"It happens when a man lies with a woman. But you needn't worry about it yet."

Maili and Catriona were silent a few minutes as they pondered this information. He was waiting for the follow on question about why the girls were with child. But it did not come this time.

"Papa Craig, is Princess not the most beautiful girl you have ever seen?" Maili said dreamily.

Gavin hesitated. "Aye, I suppose she is."

"She should be our new mama."

"Maili!" Catriona scolded.

"But why not?" Maili demanded. "She needs a husband. I heard her mama telling her papa."

"Did you? You shouldna listen to other people's conversations, lass," Gavin corrected her.

"But I could not help it. They were talking and I heard them. I was not trying to hear them." She pouted.

"All right, lass." He patted her on the head.

"Her papa said he was counting on the good doctor's charms. I hope he meant you."

Gavin could not think of a reply to satisfactorily express his feelings.

CHAPTER 5

*M*argaux saw her parents off that morning with more confidence than she felt. The house seemed empty with them gone. She would miss her parents, but their disagreement was never about them personally, she reflected. It was about what they thought was best for her, combined with a lack of desirable suitors. After determining the orphanage had no need of her services that morning, she returned to the house to forge a plan. She had miscalculated, certainly. There was less to occupy her time here than she had presumed, but she would not lose hope before her parents had passed the first mile to London.

She was also lonely; she had to confess it, at least in private, but not so lonely she would race back south. Her sister Jolie loved the *ton*, but Margaux had never enjoyed the stares and the gossip once the *ton* had assumed she had been jilted. She had certainly been the one to back out of the understanding with Lord Vernon, but it was not because she wished to. She might be many things, but she had not been able to bear marrying Lord Vernon when she had realized his affections were attached elsewhere.

She was already becoming morose. She mustn't panic. If she kept herself busy, she would not dwell on her disappointments. She searched the house for things she would find useful with which to teach the Douglas girls. She might have to send for some supplies, unless they were to be found in the nursery at the castle. She had not discussed with Lord Craig where the lessons were to take place, but she could not simply appear at the castle. Or could she? She wrinkled her face in thought. Were the rules as stringent in the country—remote Scotland—as they were in London? They were not in France.

Should she find Aunt Ida and drag her out for a small errand? She could ride over there and ask the housekeeper discreetly and be on her way. Besides, if she were to be a spinster, she did not need a chaperone. She needed to embrace her new role in life.

That was easier said than done. She could not break two decades' worth of breeding and schoolroom indoctrination with regard to calling on a bachelor, especially unchaperoned. She went in search of Aunt Ida.

Margaux could not find her aunt, and the staff did not seem to be alarmed at Ida's apparently frequent wanderings. She always returned from her walks, they said. Margaux reluctantly sat and darned more socks until Ida returned. When the darning was completed, she wrote out some French lessons and some ideas for other essentials for young ladies to learn. That occupied no more than half an hour. She walked to the window and gazed out over the beauty of the land and water. From this side of the house, she could just see the Firth of Clyde off in the distance. From the next, she could see the loch. She inhaled a deep, relaxing breath. This was why she was here. She would need to adjust her pace of life and her expectations. She had never excelled in idleness, so she had learned to manage the household with her mother from an early age. She needed to revel in the beauty around her. She wanted to be here, but she must find a way to keep her restlessness at bay. Once she made it through the first day, she was certain everything would settle into place.

∼

Gavin rode to the vicarage the next morning to call on the vicar's wife. The vicar had seemed like a sombre fellow at the funeral; not necessarily someone he would choose to spend excess amounts of time with, but not overly offensive. He was prosy, with a dour disposition that was unfortunate in a man of the cloth.

Gavin left his horse at the stable and made his way to the front door. His knock was answered by a severe woman—for there was no other way to describe her. She was dressed in unrelieved black without ornamentation, her hair was pulled back into a tight knot and her face was frozen in a scowl. Was he at the right place? His eyes glanced sideways to the church to be sure. He stood there, waiting for her to speak, but she continued to stare.

"Pardon me, but I am looking for the vicar's wife. Is Mrs. Mulligan home?"

She eyed him warily.

"I am the new Lord Craig. I have come to ask for her assistance," he explained.

The lady frowned and muttered under her breath. Gavin could not make out her speech clearly, but he thought he heard the words sinner and repent.

"The vicar is not home, but I suppose I will hear what you have to say." She stepped back and directed him into a small parlour, then she walked away. He stood in amazement. He had been calling on the sick for years and had never encountered such treatment anywhere. Gavin wondered if he was only allowed in because he provided their living. He was certain she would have slammed the door in his face otherwise. He stood in the cold room, which was devoid of any warm feeling. There were none of the signs of home that often adorned a parlour—no pictures, flowers, sewing—only a few chairs, a small table and a Bible.

Mrs. Mulligan returned with a maid, and stood inside the door staring at him. There was no offer to sit or take tea, as had been the custom in Alberfoyle. It seemed wrong in a vicarage. Had his brother tolerated this? People of God should be kind-hearted, welcoming, tender—not those you were afraid to talk to. Never one to make up his mind without more information, Gavin hoped she was simply out of sorts for some reason.

"Thank you for seeing me, Mrs. Mulligan," he began, feeling unusually tongue-tied.

She gave a slight nod.

"As you ken, my brother and his family recently perished and I have taken over his duties." He stated the obvious.

"Yes."

Gavin hesitated. If he were not desperate, he would have made his excuses and left. "We have the annual solstice ball in a few weeks, and as there is no Lady Craig, I was hoping you could help me. Or suggest someone who would be willing." He let out a breath.

Mrs. Mulligan looked at him disapprovingly by narrowing her eyes further.

"So you mean to continue on as your brother did, then? I do not approve of such frivolity, nor of pagan celebrations."

"I see," he said quietly.

"However, I will discuss the situation with the ladies' committee. Perhaps we can help put together the baskets for the tenants, but I will have no part in the ball."

"I understand." He did not really, but what else could he say? How had this miserable vicarage come to pass in his brother's parish? Iain was one of the most jovial people he had ever known.

"I will call on you later this week, with the vicar, to inform you of the committee's decision," she said curtly.

"Verra well, I am grateful for your assistance." Gavin bowed and took his leave, thankful to be out of such an absurd situation. He wished he could take his words back. He did not want her help. He did not ever want to see her again. He mounted his roan and made his way back to his property, shaking his head.

~

It was with dread that Gavin went to church the next morning. The girls were none the wiser about the rare treat in store for them, he thought, somewhat shamefully. He hoped he could avoid Mrs. Mulligan, though he doubted she would wish to converse with him either. How strange it felt to be reluctant to attend church. He hoped the lady would be pleasanter this morn. He did find it odd that none of the household had been expecting his attendance at the services this morning. When had Iain's family stopped going and why? It made no sense to Gavin.

Catriona and Maili skipped ahead of him as they chose to walk on the clear, bright morning. Both girls picked wild flowers along the way and the spaniels trotted alongside. The dogs had taken a liking to Maili and followed her everywhere. They would not appreciate sitting outside the church, but he did not think the vicar or his wife would look favourably upon canines filling the pews or floor.

They were not the first to arrive in the small stone church, and many heads turned with looks of surprise upon their entrance. Gavin smiled and shook hands with those he knew from decades past and introduced them to his wards. He would make the others' acquaintance in time. He found the old family pew and directed the girls to sit down. Before long, the crowd began to whisper and turn their heads again. It could only mean Lady Margaux and Lady Ida had arrived, he thought. He had to force his face to remain impassive. For weeks to come there would be gossip in the village about the London beauty retiring to the Scottish countryside and claiming spinsterhood. He would support her decision as best he could. He knew it was hard for women who desired independence.

Maili was tugging on his sleeve. "Papa Craig," she whispered urgently.

"Shh, lass." The vicar was walking toward the lectern.

"Princess!" Nearly shouting the word, Maili waved vigorously at her idol.

Gavin was afraid to look lest the congregation misconstrue the relationship. However, Maili had surely fanned the fire already. Look, he did, against his better judgement, and there was Lady Margaux, walking gracefully down the aisle with a pleasing smile. Alone. Unchaperoned. She seemed oblivious to the stares and murmurs. Or perhaps, with her exotic beauty, she was accustomed to it wherever she went. She was attired with the utmost propriety, in a pale blue, sprigged muslin gown. She stood out like a rose amongst thorns.

She gave a quick smile and greeting to them and sat in the pew across the aisle, then proceeded to open her prayer book with her attention focused on the vicar. Gavin knew, after his meeting with the stiff, prudish Mrs. Mulligan yesterday, it would not bode well for Lady Margaux's future here. Perhaps Lady Ida was ill, or perhaps she did not attend the Sunday services. He hoped the congregation would merely be grateful Lady Margaux was in attendance, but she was young, beautiful and unmarried. Not to mention French. Those were sins in themselves.

The service was agony. Gavin could not bring himself to concentrate on the dry, interminable monologue. He had never found an abundance of enlightenment from Leviticus and Jewish laws about laws. Maili was restless. Catriona had fallen asleep. Gavin kept thinking about the thousands of things necessary to keep the estate running. Two hours later, the congregation was finally dismissed. Gavin wondered ungraciously how they kept the pews from being empty every Sunday.

After the service, many of the parishioners greeted him with civility and passed on their condolences. No one spoke to Lady Margaux, other than Catriona and Maili. Londoners would have called it being given the cut direct. Did Lady Margaux notice? She was holding her head high while chatting and smiling at the girls. He made his excuses and walked over to greet her.

"Good day, Lady Margaux. Is Lady Ida unwell?" Gavin spoke a bit louder than normal, for he knew they had a captive audience. He hoped the congregation would realize she was not living unchaperoned.

"No, my lord." She gave him a shy smile. She leaned closer and whispered, "She cannot abide the vicar and his wife."

"I am all sympathy." However, that would not do well to warm the parishioners to her. He made idle talk with Lady Margaux, hoping some would ask for an introduction, but none came. "Did you ride here alone?"

"I was driven in the carriage with my maid, though she refused to come in."

"Shall I see you to it?" he offered.

She gave a slight nod. "Thank you."

He had not missed the slight look of disappointment in her eyes. She had noticed. He escorted her to the carriage where a footman and coachmen were waiting. He handed her into the conveyance.

"We will see you on the morrow," he said and closed the door.

He smiled and turned back toward the churchyard to be met by disapproving stares. He ignored them and led the girls home, with the spaniels following along.

As they made their way back to the castle, the sun burst through the clouds, turning the day into one too rare and glorious to spend inside.

"Girls, what say you to a picnic by the loch? Perhaps I can teach you to fish?"

Catriona looked wary.

"Would we have to touch them?" she asked cautiously.

"Aye. And I would show you how to bait the hooks. Seamus always enjoyed it, and I thought you might, too."

"Seamus delights in all manner of disgusting things," Catriona said, wrinkling her nose.

Gavin chuckled. "Aye. 'Tis part of the profession, I suppose. How about you, Maili? Are you game for some fishing?"

"I like worms," she said proudly. "I'm not afraid to touch them like Catriona is."

"Verra well. You can bait hers for her."

"Papa Craig," Maili said. She started every thought with his name, he noticed.

"Yes, lass?"

"Why didn't anyone speak to Princess at church? She seemed sad, even though she was smiling."

Gavin sighed. Children were frighteningly astute at times.

"I doona ken, lass. It made me sad that no one talked to her."

"Our vicar always said we should make everyone feel welcome in God's house," Catriona added.

"Maybe we should invite her to our picnic to make her feel better," Maili suggested.

"That is verra kind, lass. Perhaps we should."

They stepped into the entry hall and handed their bonnets and hat to Tallach.

"Girls, would you please ask Cook to pack a hamper for us, while I send a message inviting Lady Ida and Lady Margaux to join us?"

The girls nodded with excitement and ran off on their errand.

Before long, Lady Ida and Lady Margaux arrived in a gig, and they followed the Craig party down to the loch. The day had grown warmer since they had left church, so the party unfolded their blankets under the shade of a large oak.

"Thank you for the invitation, Lord Craig. It is a lovely day for a picnic," Lady Margaux said graciously.

Lady Ida simply smiled as he greeted her.

"'Tis much too lovely to be inside. One never ken how many days like this there will be in Scotland," Gavin agreed. "Now shall we eat or fish first?"

"I am famished!" Maili stated.

"Then by all means let us see what is in the hampers," Lady Margaux suggested, taking charge in a manner as natural as it was instinctive. "Will the two of you help me, please?"

Catriona and Maili eagerly sat on the blanket next to Lady Margaux and awaited her command.

"Shall we begin practising our French? Now is as good a time as any." She smiled.

"Yes," the girls said.

"*Oui*," Margaux corrected.

"*Oui*," they echoed.

She handed them plates, silver, and glasses.

"*Plaques, argenterie, tasses*," Lady Margaux instructed and the girls repeated after her as they handed out each item.

"*Jambon, fromage, pain*," she said with a smile as the girls roughly attempted to pronounce ham, cheese, and bread. "*Et, limonade*," she finished as she poured the lemonade and handed it to the girls.

"*Merci*," Gavin said handsomely as they handed him his fare.

"What does mer-see mean?" Catriona asked.

"It means thank you," Lady Margaux replied.

"*Très bien.*" Lady Ida applauded the girls.

"It means very good," Gavin said before they asked. He had enjoyed his luncheon, and wished every day could be as pleasant as this. Even simple tasks seemed easier when he wasn't alone.

"How do you like your new home thus far, girls?" Lady Margaux asked.

Maili put a finger on her chin and thought. "I like it, but I miss the people from Alberfoyle, too."

"I am certain you do. I miss my family when we are apart, but this is my new home, so I hope to find new things to like here as well." She reached out and patted Maili's hand lovingly. "How about you, Miss Catriona?"

"I want to go back. I hate it here!" Catriona said in a rare outburst of emotion.

"Catriona, that was uncalled for," Gavin said calmly.

Catriona hurried to her feet and ran off.

"Not ladylike at all, my dear," Lady Ida added in a rare moment of verbosity.

Lady Margaux spoke as she saw Gavin beginning to stand. "Give her a few moments. I remember being her age. Talking to her at the moment will do little good."

"Verra well. I imagine you ken more about females at that age than I do."

"Yes, my parents had three of us at once to deal with!" She laughed.

"Why don't you take Maili to fish, and I will speak with Catriona when she has had time to calm down."

"Thank you," Gavin said softly. He knew he should deal with Catriona, and would have to eventually, but he would take the easy way out this time.

Gavin took Maili to his favourite rock where he had fished as a boy, and taught her to bait and cast her line. He watched Lady Margaux walk over to where Catriona sat on a wooden swing dangling from a large willow. The child's head was lowered to her chest.

By the time Maili had caught and released a small fish, Gavin saw Lady Margaux returning, with her arm around Catriona, to where Aunt Ida was napping.

"Shall we return and brag about your first fish?" Gavin asked Maili.

"Yes! I think I would like to go on the swing," she said, abandoning her pole and running towards the group.

"Glad to ken I haven't lost my touch with the ladies," he muttered sarcastically to himself.

By the time he had gathered the fishing poles and walked back, Catriona was pushing Maili on the swing.

"You should row with Margaux in the boat," Lady Ida suggested, with a none-too-subtle wink.

Gavin smiled and looked at Lady Margaux, who was also amused by her aunt's ploy. She gave a slight lift of her shoulder.

"Can we row to the island I see over there?" She pointed to one of the many in the loch.

"You are certain you do not mind watching the girls?" he asked Lady Ida.

She waved her hand. "I can manage. If they misbehave, I will throw them in the water," she said with a straight face. "We can make daisy chains."

"Verra well." Gavin laughed. "Shall we?" He held out his arm for Lady Margaux.

As they walked to the small dock, Lady Margaux reassured him.

"They will come to no harm. I should not think she would wander off."

Gavin looked down at her. "Wander off?"

"Yes, she tends to wander about all day, but she always comes back."

"I feel strangely comforted. I had best row quickly. It seems there is more than my male pride at stake," he teased.

She patted his arm in a condescending fashion. "I can row if you tire. I used to race my brother, Charles."

Gavin chuckled. "I might take you up on that. The island appears much closer than it is."

Having assisted Lady Margaux into the small rowing boat, Gavin pulled on the oars and steered a course towards Creinch Island, the closest and one of the smallest that the loch boasted. As he toiled in a steady rhythm, Gavin mused about the ironic situation he now found himself in. One of the most beautiful, eligible ladies in the kingdom was in a small rowing boat with him, in what many would consider the ultimate romantic setting, and he needed a wife. However much Lady Margaux might believe she would remain a spinster, he was certain her parents would only indulge her so long before sweeping her back to London. This afternoon together had almost made him forget they were worlds apart. Yet they had some similarities which made talking to her comfortable. He actually liked Lady Margaux.

"You are rather deep in thought," she said, watching him with knowing eyes.

"I beg your pardon," he said, not masking the humour in his voice.

"Were you perhaps considering the absurdity of the situation?"

"Which part? I certainly see the irony in it," he remarked.

"Both of us jilted by the same couple, neither of us wishes to marry, yet we find ourselves together in remote Scotland?"

"Something of that nature," he agreed, feeling his eyes crinkle at the corners.

"And either by default or compassion, you find yourself often in my company."

"I would call it neither of those things. I enjoy your company."

She cocked an uncertain brow at him, but when he did not elaborate, gave a nod of thanks.

"My mother might actually swoon to see me thus." She laughed. "I wonder what she told Aunt in order to play matchmaker."

"It was Maili's idea to invite you."

"True, but would you have thought to row me about without her suggestion?"

"Perhaps."

Lady Margaux looked out over the water and appeared deep in thought.

"Why is it that the world feels marriage to be necessary for validation? Neither of our circumstances require us to marry for financial reasons." She held up her hands. "Forget that I asked. The answers will only frustrate me."

He laughed.

"At least we have each other to empathize with."

"Yes, but I am afraid it will not be for long," he said mournfully.

She looked at him in surprise. "Oh?"

"I must take a wife."

"You must?" she asked doubtfully. "Oh, you will need an heir. Please do not tell *Maman*."

"She has already suggested I need a wife. As did my steward, my housekeeper, the girls…"

"I am surprised my mother did not suggest me." She laughed.

"She was rather tactful about the entire situation," he recalled.

"That is shocking," Lady Margaux said.

"But there are too many duties for me to take on alone. Perhaps if I had been raised to run a large estate, the matter would be different. And perhaps, if I hadn't taken on the girls…" He ran his hand through his hair. "But no matter. I always wanted a family and now I have one."

"I will help you with the girls. You need not sacrifice yourself. You will eventually find a new steward and a governess." Her tone was reassuring.

"But how many will suffer in the meantime? I am as a newborn babe. And while your intentions are appreciated, I cannot expect you to fulfil these duties. I expect that, after a time, you will grow tired of being here alone."

"No," she said emphatically. "I would do anything not to be forced into an arranged marriage."

Gavin agreed; the thought of marrying a stranger was equally unwelcome to him, but he would do it for the girls and the estate. He glanced back toward the shore to check on his daughters' well-being. Lady Ida was napping on the blanket.

"I think her body is going through its natural changes," Lady Margaux said following his eyes to Catriona.

"Ah. She must be missing her mother very much at the moment, then," he said, feeling a rush of understanding.

"Yes, I believe she is embarrassed to approach you, even though you are a doctor."

"I understand the anatomical phenomenon, but I have never experienced it, of course. I am verra grateful to you for talking to her."

"What are neighbours for?"

"Indeed." *But for how long*? he asked himself again. He would have to settle for whatever help she was willing to give for the time she was allowed to remain.

"Do you think the village is always so welcoming to strangers?" she asked sardonically.

"I doona remember them being so unfriendly."

"But you grew up here," she pointed out.

"Aye. They will come about. Once you have been introduced and they realize you are here to stay."

"I hope so," she agreed quietly.

Gavin nodded to another boat passing by as they rowed back toward the shore.

"You will meet more of local society at the Squire's tomorrow evening."

"Yes, it is difficult to cut people once they are acquaintances," she said acerbically.

When they drew close to the shore, Lady Ida was splashing about in the water with the girls, their skirts tied above their knees. Lady Margaux sighed audibly. He tried not to laugh.

"Very ladylike, Aunt," Lady Margaux teased with unsuppressed humour.

"Shall we see what Cook packed for dessert?" Gavin suggested.

They climbed from the boat and proceeded to indulge in Cook's jam tarts, before Maili fell asleep and they went their separate ways.

CHAPTER 6

*M*argaux could not remember the last time she had been nervous about going into any society, let alone local, small village society. Perhaps, if she were honest, she had been a little anxious before her own début in London. At least her sisters had shared the stage with her on that occasion. Here, she was to meet the high society of the area, as befitted her new status, which would make her new home pleasant or miserable. She tried to tell herself she would be content to live in seclusion and not socialize with the neighbours at all. Maybe she would be, but it went against human nature not to desire acceptance.

She wore her emerald green satin gown. She had never fancied herself in virginal white, and she was making a statement tonight. She prayed that by arriving with Lord Craig and Lady Ida, it would pave the way for a more pleasant welcome than she had received in church, even though originally the invitation had been extended to her parents.

She knew Lord Craig was here to survey his options for a wife amongst the ladies of the neighbourhood, and she was hoping to establish herself on her own. Nevertheless, she was grateful he had offered to accompany them tonight.

The manor was more modern than Castle Craig or Breconrae. Boasting three extensive wings and two-storeyed, mullioned windows, it was a large, well-proportioned house, surrounded by manicured gardens. The interior was elegant, and was already crowded with guests.

Greeted cautiously by the hosts, Squire and Mrs. McDougal, Margaux immediately sensed she was not welcome, though they uttered the normal niceties. Lord Craig led his party on into the drawing room and chose seats for them along the aisle toward the centre of the room. Margaux again felt the disdain of haughty stares, and wondered how she could be made to feel smaller in a cramped Scottish drawing room than a London ballroom. Was there any place on earth where she would fit in?

Thankfully, the music began and Margaux was soon lost in the pleasure of Beethoven's *Moonlight Sonata*. She had not, of late, spent enough time with her violin. She would remedy that soon by indulging in her favourite hobby. The second act was a soprano, whom Margaux recognized vaguely from London. A Miss Davis, she thought, searching her memory. Their eyes met, and the soprano's appeared to narrow. How strange, Margaux reflected. She could not recollect having had so much as a conversation with the girl before, so she dismissed the look to her imagination.

When the intermission arrived, Lord Craig left to procure refreshment, and to Margaux's astonishment, she was approached by her most ardent and persistent of suitors in London, Sir Thomas Ashley-Long. Sir Thomas was a leader of the Corinthian set, who thought as highly of himself as did the fawning puppies who followed him about, attempting to copy his physical prowess. He had proposed to Margaux three times, and seemed to find sport in trying new ways to convince her. He did not appear to comprehend the meaning of the word 'no'. She suspected he had been the one to label the triplets with their nicknames, and he frequently delighted in teasing her with hers. She could not imagine it was coincidence that found him in her vicinity now.

Why ever would someone persist in their attentions when it had been made very plain they were most unwelcome? She could surmise no other reason than it offered him sport, for there were dozens of beautiful débutantes who had thrown out lures to him.

"Lady Margaux, what a delightful surprise, to be sure. I am overcome with astonishment to find you in Scotland, of all places!" Sir Thomas said dramatically, reaching for her hand, which she reluctantly gave to prevent herself from appearing rude.

"Sir Thomas. I assure you there is no greater surprise than mine. My family has an estate here, so my presence is quite natural."

"Breathing fire so early in the evening, my dragon?" he asked with an amused affection that only served to irritate her. "My sister and I are visiting our cousins who live near Ballach." He seated himself comfortably next to her and twirled his quizzing glass.

"I am surprised anything could compel you to leave London before the Season had ended," Margaux retorted.

"Are you, dear Fire?" He looked at her with the hint of condescension which never failed to infuriate her. She did not know why he bothered her so much. He was a fine specimen of a man, but he always talked to her in a manner that inferred she was already his and he was indulging her by waiting for her acceptance.

"Would you be kind enough to take a turn about the terrace with me?" He stood and held out his arm.

Margaux hesitated. He would likely persist in harassing her unless she humoured him.

"Very well." She turned to her aunt, who was staring blankly again. "Aunt, I will return shortly."

Aunt Ida smiled and nodded before returning to her favourite spot along the wall. Margaux took Sir Thomas's arm and went with him to the terrace. She saw Lord Craig talking to Miss Davis as she left. Mayhap the narrowed eyes had had meaning after all.

"Where are Lord and Lady Ashbury?" Sir Thomas questioned.

Margaux bit her lip before answering. "They have returned to London." Boldly, she looked into his eyes, daring him to accuse her of hiding.

"I see. You are here alone, then."

"No, I am with my aunt," she said defiantly.

"On a repairing lease?" Both his tone and words mocked her.

"I am here to stay."

His face broke into a knowing smile. "Ah. So you preferred someone else to me and he abandoned you."

"No!" she insisted.

"If you won't have me for a husband, perhaps we could make other arrangements." His voice husky with salacious intent. Sliding his arms around her, he pulled her to him.

"Oh, I beg your pardon!"

Margaux heard a female voice as she struggled to pull out of Sir Thomas's embrace. This was certainly not how she would make a good impression in the locality.

"It is not what you think," Sir Thomas said to Miss Davis, who eyed Margaux with distaste.

Margaux wanted to laugh. Now he did not wish to have her for a wife. Then she heard the music begin and she could have wept. Now her shame was witnessed and she would be seen walking in late to the drawing room. Miss Davis had already returned there, and she was left alone with Sir Thomas again.

She turned to go back and face the disapprobation, whereupon he reached out for her.

"Margaux, don't go. I apologize!" he called after her as she evaded his grasp and slipped through a back door and made for the retiring room.

She stayed there some time until her anger had cooled. Hopefully, by now, Sir Thomas had returned to the main gathering and no one would associate her absence with his. She gathered her courage and returned to the drawing room. The music had ended and she glanced around for her aunt. Her eyes met Lord Craig's, as Miss Davis flitted her fan flirtatiously in front of him. As Margaux stood at the edge of the room, she overheard loud whispers.

"The poor girl must not know any better. I hear she is French and they have notoriously loose ways. Coming here dressed like an opera dancer..." a haughty female voice said.

"I hear she was ruined in London and came here to hide," another voice said in a confiding whisper.

"I am astonished she has the brass to show her face in public. She even went to church alone! And then again, she was seen out on the loch alone with a man."

She'd had a maid with her at church even if she was in the carriage, she thought indignantly. Word certainly spread quickly in the country!

"I am thankful Thomas had a narrow escape! He was dangling after her in London. How was I to know? She is the daughter of a marquess." The woman clucked.

Margaux did not want to hear any more. She should have expected this. She held up her head and walked right past the gossiping harridans, muttering in French for their benefit.

"Imbéciles! Un groupe inutile de commères!"

They all considered her ruined. If word got back to London—which of course it would—her parents would come straight back and try to make her leave. Not that she gave a fig what these biddies thought, but she would not easily be able to stay here alone. Was there anything she could do to save her reputation? In London, marriage was the only way. Sometimes a repairing lease would answer—but she was already on one. There had to be a way, or she would be married off to one of the London suitors. Her mother was a force to be reckoned with in the *ton*, but would that be enough? Was Lord Craig aware of the gossip? She walked toward him, her head high, pretending nothing was wrong.

"Lord Craig, would it trouble you to escort us home?" she asked politely with a smile.

"Of course not, lass. I will call for the carriage, if you care to bring Lady Ida to the entrance hall."

"Thank you."

She wondered if she should she tell him what had transpired on the way home or wait for him to hear the gossip? Now, where was Aunt Ida?

∾

The next day, from his study, Gavin spotted a gig drawing in through the gates of the castle. He wondered who could be visiting at this hour. Perhaps the vicar was out on his rounds. He cut across the lawn to meet the carriage.

He was astonished to find Lady Margaux and Lady Ida climbing down from the vehicle.

"Good morning, Lord Craig," Lady Margaux said with a cheerful smile, taking his extended hand.

"Good morning, ladies. This is a pleasant surprise." He bowed to each of them.

Lady Ida held out her hand. "Who are you?" she asked with a vacant gaze.

"This is Lord Craig, Aunt Ida, remember?"

"Why, no. I would remember that face. I am pleased to meet you, sir." She held out her hand and smiled flirtatiously.

He held back a laugh and he kissed her hand. At least she was pleasantly demented.

"Forgive us for calling uninvited," Lady Margaux said, "but we did not settle if your girls would come to me or I would come to them for lessons today."

"I beg your pardon, I had not thought," Gavin said. "There are many things for me to learn."

"It is no bother. I was planning which lessons to do with them and thought to search the nursery here for supplies."

"I am verra grateful to you," he said. "Please make yourself at home. I will tell Mrs. Ennis to make you welcome. And do not listen to what she says of me as a boy. It is not true." He laughed.

"I cannot imagine you as anything other than charming." He observed Lady Margaux blush when she realized what she had said. "I am sorry. I did not mean to..."

"I took it the way intended. Let me send for the girls." Gavin turned and led the way to the small back parlour and rang for the girls to be brought down.

"Lady Margaux!" Catriona shrieked.

"Princess!" She and Maili came over to greet her.

"Good morning, Catriona and Maili." Lady Margaux gave a small curtsy, which they dutifully returned, looking somewhat shamefaced at their lack of manners.

"Have you come to dance?"

"I am afraid not. We will have to arrange for either a dancing master or someone to play. There must be music or someone to show you the steps," Lady Margaux explained.

The girls frowned in disappointment.

"I doona play, girls. I'm sorry," Gavin said at their obvious sadness.

"I play." From her chair by the window, Lady Ida spoke up.

Gavin and Lady Margaux looked at each other with surprise.

"You do?" Lady Margaux asked sweetly.

"Of course. I do not remember much else." Lady Ida stood and looked around for something. "Where is that pianoforte?"

Gavin smothered a chuckle. "I suspect it was taken off to the music room. Shall we go and see?"

The girls jumped up and down excitedly and followed them out.

They found the room, which looked as if it had not seen much use. Iain's boys had been much keener on fishing and riding, Gavin remembered.

Lady Ida sat down at the piano and began to plunk out some tunes. Gavin had seen cases where memory loss had occurred with respect to new things rather than old. If Lady Ida had played for countless hours as a girl, it could account for her ability to remember.

She stopped and looked up. "Are you going to dance?"

"Show us how, Princess," Maili exclaimed.

Lady Margaux looked towards Gavin to see if he was willing. "Shall we?"

"I would love to see a waltz," Catriona said dreamily.

"A waltz? But it will be many years before you may do such a thing. Why not learn a simple country dance first?" Lady Margaux suggested.

"Please? Just to watch?" Catriona pleaded.

"I can waltz with you, lass, if you've no objection?" Gavin had always enjoyed dancing. He had learned to waltz whilst staying with the Eastons, who were a merry bunch.

"None," Lady Margaux said, but looked surprised. "I wonder if Aunt knows any to play." She appeared to think for a moment. "Aunt Ida, do you know any songs in three-quarter time?"

"Why, certainly."

Surprisingly, Lady Ida began the Viennese waltz, and Gavin gathered Lady Margaux's hand and placed his arm on her waist. In that moment, everything changed. With her touch, he was awakened from his trance-like existence. He would be cold-blooded if he did not acknowledge his reaction to her. Even though he had been told he was handsome, he had always been intimidated by beauty such as hers. She was beautiful and elegant in a way he was not. But in this moment, he felt different in her company. He needed to divert his thoughts quickly. He had not felt this way since Lady Beatrice. He had thought that part of him was dead. They were friends.

"I do not know if waltzing fits with my new spinster role," Lady Margaux said with a laugh, interrupting his thoughts.

"I think you will have a difficult time as a spinster, to be honest, lass. It seemed as if one of your suitors may have followed you here."

"It is to be hoped he realized his mistake last night," she said, with a crease between her brows.

"Was he inappropriate on the terrace?" Gavin asked, his forehead crinkling into a concerned frown.

"Sir Thomas is harmless. Unfortunately, your Miss Davis came upon him trying to convince me of his charms."

"So that was what she was trying to hint at," Gavin said thoughtfully.

"She had the nerve to tell you that? I should not be surprised. She was giving me looks when she saw me sitting with you. No doubt you are accustomed to females throwing themselves at you."

"Aye. I'm afraid so." He chuckled. "It became obvious to me as a doctor, when I would be called upon over and over for suspicious ailments. It was good for my practice though."

"Do you realize, that now you are titled with property, it will only be worse? Did you notice the birds circling last evening?" she asked teasingly.

"I confess I had hoped I would find a candidate for the position of Lady Craig."

"Were you successful?"

He shook his head. "I'm afraid not. The only one who might have suited became ineligible when she attempted to malign you."

"I am much obliged, Lord Craig, but you must not feel the need to fight my battles for me. I knew there would be some talk when I assumed a life of independence, but I underestimated how quickly gossip spreads and takes on a life of its own."

He looked down at her. "Did something else happen last night?"

"I overheard the matrons gossiping about me when I returned from the retiring room. It was not kind. They consider me to be ruined and hiding here."

"Rubbish!" he exclaimed.

"Therefore, you may not want to be seen in my presence, or for it to be known that I am teaching your daughters," she warned.

"They can go hang. I do not need their society."

Lady Margaux ignored his chivalry and sighed. "My parents will try to force me to marry now, if anyone will still have me."

"We could help each other and marry," he said, in partial jest.

"Do be serious, I beg of you. Let us enjoy the dance."

That was a colossal mistake. Talking had been a welcome distraction from his disastrous thoughts. He needed to think logically about his future, not with emotion and feeling, especially with someone who did not wish for his attentions. Although, could that be a good thing?

After the waltz, he stayed and watched Lady Margaux teach the girls a country dance. She was wonderful with them. They adored her. Would she possibly consider? He needed a wife, and she more than fitted his needs. He knew she would have difficulty as a spinster. Yesterday's musicale and the church service were perfect examples of why. She would never be accepted as an independent woman here, though she was stubborn enough to try to brazen it out. Perhaps if she thought the alternative worse, she would accept an offer. It would be difficult to have a marriage of convenience, but they were becoming friends, and perhaps one day she might have more than friendly affection for him.

Gavin felt as if he would be a good husband. He would certainly never ask her to do anything she was not comfortable with. Although he admitted it would be difficult to be near Lady Margaux and not have her, now that he felt attracted to her.

Would it be uncomfortable if she said no? His girls would miss her. He desperately needed her help, but he was not certain if it would remain possible were she not his wife. With the gossip last night, she would be ostracized if she spent any more time alone with him. Would his protection be enough? If it were widely spread that she was ruined, she would be hunted by unrespectable offers.

The music stopped, interrupting his thoughts. "That is all for today, girls. I think perhaps we should have our lessons at Breconrae tomorrow," Lady Margaux suggested.

"Must we be done?" Catriona asked.

"This has been the best day of my life!" Maili exclaimed and gave Lady Margaux a hug.

"Run along for tea," Gavin directed whilst helping Lady Ida to stand.

"Tea sounds lovely," she agreed.

"Catriona, please take Lady Ida to the parlour. I would like to speak with Lady Margaux for a moment."

Lady Ida went off happily with the girls. Gavin turned to face Lady Margaux, who was looking at him questioningly.

"You wish to ask me something?"

"Aye." He looked took hold of her hands and looked into her eyes. "Lady Margaux, will you marry me?"

CHAPTER 7

I beg your pardon?" Had she heard him right? She had not considered he might be interested in someone like her. He had made no attempts to engage her affections. Maybe they were not as different as she had thought. She had merely thought him jesting.

"I ken it is sudden."

"Ah. A marriage of convenience? And I had imagined you a romantic, Lord Craig." Margaux barely maintained civility in her voice.

"You ken I had not thought to marry after what happened with Lady Beatrice."

She remained silent.

"I need a wife, Lady Margaux. At least you and I are not strangers. I would even dare to call you friend."

She acknowledged his words with a nod.

"After the musicale, the way the congregation behaved, and the pace at which gossip spreads, you will have to make a choice. Your parents will do whatever they must to protect you. Would you rather be forced into marrying someone you do not ken? When we were dancing, it occurred to me that we might be able to help each other. A partnership, if you will."

"So you only desire me to run your household? And to help fend off title-seeking fortune hunters?" she asked, infusing her voice with sarcasm.

"It doesna sound verra nice when you put it in such a way, but I do need your help. I thought after the musicale, you might be more receptive."

Her face relaxed. "I appreciate your honesty. You do not love me, I do not love you, but if I marry you, my parents and the villagers will be happy, while you will have a mother for your girls and someone to run your house." She held out each arm, motioning as if she were balancing a weight with each one.

"I would hope it would help you, too. I did think we were friends, and that means more to me now than only having a wife. But you are right; if you gain nothing by the arrangement, then I canna ask it of you. Forgive me for mentioning it."

"I am flattered, Lord Craig. It is just that I have always promised myself I would only marry for love," she said sadly.

"I would also prefer to marry someone I ken and respect, but I must marry soon. I canna do everything myself."

"I wish I *had* behaved badly. I haven't even done anything remotely...scandalous to warrant this treatment!" She threw up her hands in disgust.

"What do you have in mind, lass?" he asked, teasing.

"I refuse to give in when I've done nothing wrong—other than flout what they think I should do."

"I will remain your friend, Lady Margaux," he reassured.

She contemplated the situation, chewing on a strand of hair in a moment of unladylike behaviour she was not normally given to. "What about an heir?" she asked candidly at last.

Gavin looked at his feet. A faint blush tinged his cheeks at her plain speaking.

Gavin tried to control the heat rising within. Plain speaking, indeed.

"I would never force you to do anything you wouldna wish."

Margaux nodded. She knew he would be kind. The strange thing was, maybe it would not be terrible to marry him. It felt surprisingly…comfortable.

She had been repulsed by marriage because of the way society viewed it. Then, once she had realized she couldn't have what her parents did, she had turned against it. But her parents would never be happy as long as she remained unwed, and she could have a good life here; maybe even children. The thought of being pursued, even here in the country alone made her shudder as she thought back on the desperate measures men had used in London.

"May I think on it?"

He looked up sharply, surprise in his eyes.

"Of course, lass. Will you join us for dinner?"

She nodded. "Yes, I should like that. Thank you."

He walked her to the parlour for tea and to locate Aunt Ida. They took their leave shortly, and Margaux left with her thoughts in a whirl. Her heart and her mind were at odds.

Gavin watched the ladies leave with hope in his breast. Lady Margaux had not said no. He could not believe he had asked in such a precipitous fashion, but he did not regret it. Could he really have the good fortune to find a wife so soon; one who was perfectly suited to care for the girls and to run the household? And who, perhaps, might even one day learn to have affection for him? He dared not hold out false optimism, but maybe she was different from society. She had said she had wanted to marry for love. He only worried she still harboured such feelings for Lord Vernon. He could not, in all fairness, be jealous of that, he reasoned. He himself was not looking for love. She would be an answer to his prayers.

Gavin noticed a carriage pulling into the drive as Lady Margaux drove out. Who could be arriving now? The conveyance came closer and Gavin saw the vicar and his wife, both with stern looks of disapproval on their faces.

"Reverend and Mrs. Mulligan, welcome." Gavin greeted them with more cheer than he felt.

"Lord Craig," the vicar said as he helped his wife down.

"Please come in. You just missed Lady Ida and Lady Margaux. Are you acquainted?"

"We are aware of them," Mrs. Mulligan snapped.

Gavin raised a deliberate eyebrow as he led them into the drawing room.

"That is, we are familiar with Lady Ida and Lord and Lady Ashbury. We have not yet made the acquaintance of Lady Margaux or the other children," Reverend Mulligan elaborated.

"Were you aware that they are providing shelter for harlots at their so-called orphanage, Lord Craig?" Mrs. Mulligan practically spat venom.

"I beg your pardon?"

"The house is full of young women with loose morals," Mrs. Mulligan continued with distaste. "And leaving a young lady alone at a country estate can only mean *one* thing. You should guard your repu-tation, sir. It will do you no good to be seen with those *ladies*. I use the term lightly."

"I saw nothing to indicate..." Gavin said with a wrinkled brow.

"Oh, you wouldna. But trust me," she interrupted.

"It is written in the holy book of Proverbs: *He that keepeth company with harlots spendeth his substance*," Reverend Mulligan recited.

"Were you close with my brother, Vicar?" Gavin asked, ignoring the recitation.

The man cast his eyes down.

"We had a disagreement, my lord. He refused to repent."

"I see." Gavin did not know what to say, but he suddenly felt ill. He knew he must tread carefully, being new, but this surpassed all bounds.

"We do not approve of his whisky operation. I trust you will cease the work of the devil?" Mrs. Mulligan demanded.

"The devil? Is that not rather overstating the matter?"

"It is written in the book of Ephesians: *And be not drunken with wine, wherein is riot, but be filled with the Spirit,*" the vicar recited again.

"I see," Gavin said clenching his jaw for fear he would say what he was actually thinking.

"Yes, we are hoping, as the new laird, you will help our village return to God and cast out the sin that is pervading it by closing the distillery, and by helping us to convince Lord Ashbury to send the harlots away!" Mrs. Mulligan said.

The vicar seemed only capable of reciting verses, and Mrs. Mulligan was speaking with such irrational conviction, Gavin could see he would get nowhere by arguing with someone so clearly demented. The Mulligans' presence was making his skin crawl. He could think of nothing but how to rid the village of them.

"I will think on what you have said, Vicar," Gavin said, trying to keep the anger from his voice.

"We came to discuss the solstice ball. We have decided we cannot support the continuation of this celebration of paganism. You would do best to cancel the ball and observe proper mourning for your family. I assure you the village will applaud your sensibility." Mrs. Mulligan issued an ultimatum.

How long must he sit in his own house and be insulted? He understood the vicar's position to a degree, and that he felt he must preach what was on his conscience. But to imply Gavin's family practised paganism and encouraged sin and debauchery was the outside of enough—not to mention the insults hurled upon the Ashbury name and their good works. Could these people be reading the same Bible as he? He had listened to enough. He stood up.

"I am sorry you feel that way. The Craigs have been God-fearing servants all their lives. I have no intention of cancelling the ball—the ball that is put on for the villagers—or of asking Lord Ashbury to cast out the needy young women he is helping; nor yet to cease whatever business my brother had started in order to employ many of those same villagers and provide food for their tables. Is there anything else you would care to ask?"

The vicar and Mrs. Mulligan glared at him.

"We will have to wash our hands of you then, my lord. In Psalms it is written: *Blessed is the man who walketh not in the counsel of the ungodly, nor standeth in the way of sinners, nor sitteth in the seat of the scornful.*"

"Verra well. Then may I also suggest you find another parish to preach in. Good day."

"You will regret this, Lord Craig," Mrs. Mulligan warned.

"Are you threatening me? I willna be bullied." Now he was angry. He was never angry.

"You will answer to God for your poor judgement," she said curtly.

"I will happily answer to God rather than you. Tallach will show you out."

The Mulligans left in a high dudgeon and Gavin felt sick. He had handled the situation badly, but he knew he was right. He understood why Iain had fallen out with the vicar, but why had he kept him on? Gavin found Wallace and told him of his decision, then went upstairs to change for dinner, feeling melancholy. He loathed conflict, but not quite as much as he despised self-righteous prigs who abused their privilege as men of the cloth.

Margaux spent the afternoon pacing about the garden. Eventually, she made the decision to stay busy and not dwell on Lord Craig's proposal. He did not truly want her as a wife, merely as a mother and housekeeper. Indeed, he was not stern, and she did not think he would demand anything unreasonable of her, but she still could not bring herself to marry for convenience. Her pride rebelled at the very idea. She did not see why she could not help him and maintain her independence at her father's estate. She would weather this storm.

However, when she sought out Mrs. Bailey to offer help, she was turned away yet again. This would never work if she would not be allowed to do anything. She threw up her hands in resignation, and marched back to the house. She would call on the vicar's wife. There had to be something she could do for the ladies' committee. If she showed herself a humble servant, eventually the village would open their eyes to the truth.

Aunt Ida was resting, so Margaux decided to dress in her severest spinster's dress and mob-cap before setting out alone. The world would have to accept her in this role. She travelled in the gig with a footman, at his insistence. She could deal with having him with her. Footmen often came in handy when needing to run a quick errand. In all likelihood, her father's instructions to the servants had been that she not be permitted to go out alone.

She trotted the gig through the small village and soon reached the vicarage, where she handed the reins to the footman. Jumping down lightly without assistance, she walked to the door and rapped on the knocker. No answer came, although she could hear the sounds of bustling activity, Perhaps they could not hear her. She pondered what she should do. They were obviously occupied, so it might be best to return another time. After a few moments' indecision, she finally decided to send the footman around to the back door, to enquire whether or not the vicar's wife was at home.

She paced up and down the short drive for several minutes, uncaring that she was displaying her agitation to the curious to witness. She had never been in such a place, nor had she spent time in the country. And never alone.

At last the footman returned, but he had a strange look on his face.

"Is something the matter?" she asked.

He hesitated.

"You can tell me. I will not bite," she said with a smile, trying to make him feel at ease.

"The missus be home, but she'llna see ye."

"Pardon?" Had she heard correctly?

His face turned red. He was clearly embarrassed.

"I'd rather not repeat wha' she said, m'lady," he said looking down at his feet.

"Very well," she answered. She did not want to make him more uncomfortable than he already was. "Could you perhaps give me an approximation?"

"I think she doona approve of the housing of ruined girls at Breconrae, nor your reputat'n."

"I see. Let us leave, then." She would not allow her disgust to show. "I need to purchase a few things in the village."

"Aye, m'lady."

Margaux vowed she would find a way. She would not give up on her plans so easily. She was disturbed by the fact that the vicar had judged her before meeting her, but she hoped the rest of the village would be more accepting. She would not hold her breath, however, after her reception at the Squire's musical reception.

They stopped before the haberdasher's shop, and Margaux handed the reins once again to the footman.

"I shall not be long."

She walked into the small shop and was greeted with curious stares from the customers. That did not surprise her. She selected a few items to help with the lessons for Lord Craig's daughters, and decided to treat them to some new ribbons. The shopkeeper seemed a kind man, but the ladies present were whispering and giving her scornful looks. Somehow she knew, without hearing the words, that they had already heard the gossip.

Having paid for her purchases, she climbed into the gig to return home, not a little disappointed. This escape from London was not proceeding as she had hoped. She wished her parents had allowed her to go to the convent. She had no doubt that the nuns would have kept her occupied without her being the subject of ridicule, or a prey to the temptation of blue eyes.

Lifting her chin, Margaux steeled her resolve and decided not to run from this. Once they saw her constancy, they would soften.

Nevertheless, she could not help but be a bit forlorn when, on her return, she made her way upstairs to dress for dinner.

CHAPTER 8

*T*he butler led Margaux and Aunt Ida into the drawing room, where Lord Craig was waiting to greet them. His usual pleasant smile was absent. Margaux had never seen him look cross before.

"Good evening, ladies." He walked toward them and made the proper greetings, but his smile did not reach his eyes. He looked upset. Did he regret asking her to marry him? Maybe he had heard more gossip about her in the village and had decided she was not suitable.

Margaux wondered whether she should bring up her experience that afternoon or keep it to herself. She did not want to put him or his daughters in a bad situation. He would be here for the rest of his life, while she had no notion how her sojourn at Breconrae would unfold. She could not run away every time there was a problem, but her parents were unlikely to allow her to remain in Scotland unless she was able to redeem the situation.

The butler announced dinner was served and they made their way to the dining room. Once they were seated and the first course set before them, Margaux decided it was best to tell him her concerns.

"Is anything wrong, my lord? You seem somewhat distracted," she asked boldly.

"My apologies," he answered. "I had a disturbing visitation this afternoon."

"You should have sent word. We would have stayed at home this evening."

"No. I was merely debating whether or not to tell you about it."

"I was debating if I should tell you about my visit to the vicarage," she confessed.

"The vicarage? Oh no, I can imagine it," he said, his forehead wrinkling. "The vicar and his wife were my visitors today."

"Strictly speaking, I did not actually visit," she amended. "They refused to see me."

"That is probably fortunate, lass. I wish I had not seen them."

"What happened?"

"They insulted me in almost every way imaginable. They accused me of perpetuating drunkenness and demanded I cease Iain's distillery operation. They also accused me of associating with loose women, and had the effrontery to claim your orphanage was housing harlots."

"Harlots? And I am the loose woman you were accused of associating with?"

He nodded. "I'm sorry, lass. I shouldna have mentioned it." He reached over and gently touched her hand, which sent pulses of awareness through her. She had to take a breath to settle her racing heart.

"I daresay I should not go out alone. I had supposed, foolishly it seems, that by declaring myself a spinster and having Aunt Ida with me, I should avoid such tittle-tattle."

"Old harridan." Aunt Ida made a rare contribution to the conversation. "They should have been gone by now."

Lord Craig laughed. "Indeed."

"I have never had the pleasure of actually meeting Mrs. Mulligan," Margaux said.

"You willna have to. I asked them to leave," he declared.

Margaux was surprised, but pleasantly so.

"I've no idea why my brother didna dismiss him. They didna see eye to eye, either."

"Perhaps it would be best if we do not socialize unless my parents are here. You may still send your daughters to me for lessons, and I will still help you plan the ball. If your housekeeper and cook would not object to waiting on me at Breconrae, it would not be difficult."

"This is ridiculous! I willna allow some over-righteous, misinterpreting fools to dictate how I run my life, nor who I have in my home. You are always welcome here, no matter your decision."

"Thank you, my lord. However, until the village accepts me here, it would perhaps be best to observe the proprieties."

"I doona wish to pressure you, but if you lived here you would be under my protection. They willna shun you as Lady Craig."

Margaux nodded and looked down at the starched tablecloth. Lost in thought, she absently pushed her food around her plate. She knew what he said to be true. She had the overwhelming feeling of losing her first major battle in her fight. Already she was looking forward to helping Lord Craig and the girls—even to furthering her friendship with him. There was something about him that drew her to him. Of course, he was devastatingly handsome, but it would be the height of hypocrisy for her to be drawn to him for his beauty when she despised being treated in the same manner herself. However, she knew he had a point. She had seen any variety of misdeeds and sins become magically acceptable under the guise of marriage. She considered him as he attempted to talk to Aunt Ida.

Could she be happy, married to him? She thought she could. She was good at reading people, and did not believe he was playing her false. He was nothing like the men she had come to Scotland to avoid. She would have more freedom once married, if she agreed the terms from the beginning. Perhaps she would be better off than continuing her resolution to live as a spinster. Her parents might pressure her to marry someone much less desirable than Lord Craig in order to save the family reputation for her sisters' sakes. She inhaled deeply.

"Lord Craig," she said softly when there was a pause in the conversation. He looked back at her with his startling eyes and her resolve almost left her. She desperately hoped she wasn't setting herself up for heartbreak. "You have convinced me. I will marry you." She paused. "With conditions."

He reached over, took her hand and kissed it. "I will do my best to make you happy, lass, though I ken I am not who you would wish for your mate."

"Thank you." She believed him, and also felt guilty that he felt she was doing him such a favour. "When may the wedding take place? It will be some time before my parents return."

"We also happen to be lacking a clergyman at the moment," he said, with a twinkle in his eye. "Although, he is the last person I would wish to bless our union."

"We don't need clergy or banns in Scotland. Even I know that."

"True. We could say *I do* before two witnesses and be done with it."

"Let us do it, then." In for a penny, in for a pound, she reasoned to herself.

Lord Craig wrinkled his forehead. "Just because we can, it doesna mean we should. I take this marriage the same way I would any other."

In that moment, Margaux's heart softened.

"We should at least write to your parents for their blessing."

"I do not think it necessary, especially considering the gossip. They will be so grateful to you, they will likely double my dowry," she jested. Besides, she did not wish for a grand wedding at St. George's in London. Everything her mother did was grand, but that was not Margaux's style.

"I do not need a grand wedding." *Especially not for a marriage of convenience*, she thought.

"Are you certain?"

"I have no doubt my parents will approve."

"I approve," Aunt Ida chimed in, smiling warmly at them.

"Aunt Ida approves. There. Now can you find one more witness?"

Lord Craig looked concerned and sat in deep thought for a few moments.

"Verra well," he said at last. "If you will withdraw with me to the parlour, we can discuss your conditions, and then I will see who I can find for witnesses."

~

Margaux found herself alone in the parlour for some time after they had discussed her terms. Lord Craig had graciously agreed to all of her requirements about the marriage—she almost regretted having voiced her concerns as she had watched the shock on his face during the conversation. But without her father to speak for her, she had felt she must stand for her rights. She would have her independence were she widowed, there would be no consummation without mutual consent, and she would not be required to seek his permission over trivial matters. He had asked nothing of her, she recalled with guilt.

Apparently, Aunt Ida had wandered off somewhere between the parlour and the dining room. Margaux did not mind having some time to compose herself. What had she done? It had seemed a reasonable thing to do when she was staring into Lord Craig's comforting eyes, but at this moment she doubted her sanity. Was she truly about to be unequivocally, irrevocably married?

She prayed she was making the right decision. She pondered her circumstances and realized she had little choice unless she wanted to return to London. There could no longer be much of a life for her here as a spinster, alone with only her senile aunt for company, since the village would continue to shun her.

Catriona and Maili burst into the room just then, interrupting her reflections.

"Is it true?" Catriona's voice quivered with doubt.

"Are you to be our new mama?" Maili asked excitedly, while pulling on Margaux's hand.

"Yes." Margaux was too overcome to say more. She wished she shared their enthusiasm, but was determined to make the best of the situation. For herself and the girls. She remembered the gifts she had bought them at the shop that afternoon. Had that been today? It seemed as though time was moving without her and she had lost control. She called for her cloak and when the servant returned, took the small presents from a pocket.

"What do you have there?" Maili enquired with her usual fervor.

"I was in the village this afternoon and thought you would enjoy these."

She handed each girl the ribbons she had purchased for them.

Maili quickly returned hers for Margaux to place in her hair. When Margaux looked up, Catriona was still fingering her ribbon and had tears in her eyes.

"What is wrong? If you do not like the colour, we can choose another tomorrow," she said kindly.

"It is perfect. My mother used to give us ribbons, and no one has given me one since. Thank you."

"Oh, my dear." Margaux wrapped the child in a hug. "There will be lots of ribbons in your life again."

Catriona giggled.

"Your pardon, ladies, are we interrupting?" Lord Craig—Gavin—was standing at the door in his clan's colours and she almost forgot to breathe at the sight of him. Never before had she seen a man look so stunning in a kilt and she was thankful she had worn a nice gown that evening. She'd had no idea, of course, when she had chosen it, that it would be her wedding gown.

"Not at all," she answered.

"Look, Papa Craig! Mama Margaux gave us new ribbons!"

Margaux's knees almost buckled at hearing herself called Mama. It was something she would quickly have to become accustomed to.

"Verra beautiful, girls." He bent to whisper to them and they nodded, then ran out of the room.

Mrs. Ennis, who had entered in Lord Craig's wake, bobbed a curtsey. "If you please, my lady, would you accompany me into the room?"

Margaux found it curious, but did as she was bade.

Aunt Ida stood beside the fireplace holding a daisy chain she had made. At a motion of the old lady's hand, Margaux joined her and bent forward so her aunt could place the circlet on her head. She was touched by the gesture.

"Thank you."

Aunt Ida just smiled at her.

The girls came through the door carrying a mixture of flowers they must have quickly picked in the garden. Margaux chuckled lightly. It seemed everyone was determined to make it as much of a wedding as possible, despite the circumstances.

"Are you ready, m'lady?" Mrs. Ennis asked softly.

"I believe so." Ready or not, Margaux held her chin high. Aunt Ida held out her arm to escort her, and they followed the girls into the parlour at her aunt's sedate pace.

She almost recoiled when she realized the entire room was filled with Craig's servants. He must have ordered his entire staff to be present. She looked at Gavin, so handsome with his plaid across his shoulder, standing next to an old man, who was at least eighty if he was a day, and she smiled. Gavin smiled back, his expression sheepish, and she knew everything would somehow be all right. She was not marrying a cold man. He was loving and kind by nature. She would be happy. She had to be.

"I am open to offers if you do not want him," Aunt Ida whispered to her.

Margaux was too nervous to laugh. Then again, Aunt Ida might believe herself to still be a young débutante.

"I promised." Margaux decided to answer safely.

Aunt Ida passed Margaux's hand to Gavin and winked at them.

"Well, you certainly took care of the witnesses," Margaux said quietly.

"I dinna want any doubt. I am sorry your family canna be with you, but we can have a ceremony in the church—with a proper vicar —later, if you wish."

She nodded. He cared for her feelings, at least. Her family was important to her, especially her sisters. Though they were different, they were an inseparable part of her.

"Shall we begin?" the old man asked in a very thick brogue.

Margaux tilted her head at Gavin as if to ask where he had found this stranger at short notice. Gavin leaned toward her and explained. "This is my old steward, Wallace. He takes this verra seriously."

The old steward. Good heavens. And this was legal in Scotland.

"Welcome. Ye are witness to this blessed union of Lady Margaux Winslow and Lord Craig. Firstly, Mrs. Ennis wishes to speak her blessing."

The older housekeeper stood, teary-eyed with apparent happiness as one of her charges was to be wed.

"May God be with ye and bless ye.
    May ye see yer children's children.
    May ye be poor in misfortune, rich in blessings.
    May ye ken nothing but happiness,
    From this day forward."

"And now ye shall repeat the vows after me," Wallace stated, as Mrs. Ennis took her seat.

"I, Gavin Samuel Laren Craig, in the name of the spirit of God that resides within us all, by the life that courses within my blood and the love that resides within my heart, take thee Margaux Catherine Serena Winslow to my hand, my heart, and my spirit, to be my chosen one. To desire thee and be desired by thee, to possess thee, and be possessed by thee, without sin or shame, for naught can exist in the purity of my love for thee. I promise to love thee wholly and completely without restraint, in sickness and in health, in plenty and in poverty, in life and beyond, where we shall meet, remember, and love again. I shall not seek to change thee in any way. I shall respect thee, thy beliefs, thy people, and thy ways as I respect myself."

"I, Margaux Catherine Serena Winslow, in the name of the spirit of God that resides within us all, by the life that courses within my blood, and the love

that resides within my heart, take thee, Gavin Samuel Laren Craig to my hand, my heart, and my spirit to be my chosen one. To desire and be desired by thee, to possess thee, and be possessed by thee, without sin or shame, for naught can exist in the purity of my love for thee. I promise to love thee wholly and completely without restraint, in sickness and in health, in plenty and in poverty, in life and beyond, where we shall meet, remember, and love again. I shall not seek to change thee in any way. I shall respect thee, thy beliefs, thy people, and thy ways as I respect myself."

"And now for the rings."

Gavin slipped a ring into her hand. She looked at him gratefully.

"Place the ring on each other's fingers, and repeat after me..."

"I take ye my heart
At the rising of the moon
And the setting of the stars.
To love and to honour
Through all that may come.
Through all our lives together
In all our lives,
May we be reborn
That we may meet and know
And love again,
And remember."

"Miss Douglas?"

As Catriona stood and read a verse, Gavin placed a sash of his family's tartan around Margaux's neck. This felt very real. She was grateful they were not in church or she would feel a traitor for speaking her words. They had pledged their love. God would strike them down for this. She wondered what vows they used for society marriages that had been arranged. Margaux had not listened to the few ceremonies she had attended. She had not been able to hear well from where she was and was brought out of her thoughts by Catriona's words.

"Now you are bound one to the other
    With a tie not easy to break.
    Take the time of binding
    Before the final vows are made
    To learn what you need to know
    To grow in wisdom and love.
    That your marriage will be strong
    That your love will last
    In this life and beyond."

"Miss Maili?" The little girl stood up and read her verse proudly.

"A thousand welcomes to you with your marriage. May you be healthy all your days. May you be blessed with long life and peace, may you grow old with goodness, and with riches."

Gavin leaned forward and placed a chaste kiss on her lips, but whispered to her in a voice that made her weak in the knees.

"Tugaim mo chroí duit go deo."

She had no idea what it meant, but somehow she knew she was fortunate to have received his gift that day.

The servants stood and cheered as Wallace pronounced them man and wife: Lord and Lady Craig. The retainers each offered their congratulations, leaving Wallace and Aunt Ida to the last to add their names as witness to the union.

"A couple must consummate a marriage in Scotland," Aunt Ida remarked.

Margaux fought a blush.

"She is right," Wallace agreed cheerfully, and slapped Gavin heartily on the back.

"It is not necessary tonight, however," Gavin said to her. "I will send for you and your belongings tomorrow. You may have tonight to rest—unless you wish to remain here…"

"No, tomorrow would be perfect. Thank you," she said gratefully. It gave her a little more time to come to terms with what had happened.

"We can arrange a proper wedding breakfast and ball once I have sent a post to your family."

Aunt Ida and Margaux took their leave right away. She did not care to linger that night. When they returned to Breconrae, she made her way to her room and to bed. Marriages had been arranged for centuries, after all. It was no different from the lot of most other ladies in society and she did have the luxury of an acquaintance with Lord Craig, albeit a brief one. She collapsed on to the bed, too tired to face her thoughts of self-betrayal that night.

She slept fitfully, and had a horrid nightmare she could not wake from. The house was engulfed in flames and she could not find a way out of her room. The room was too hot to bear; her skin felt as though it were melting and her throat as if she were drawing breath through a muffler.

She heard her name being called, but her eyes refused to open. She was growing weary in her dream, and only wished to return to undisturbed sleep. It felt like something was searing her arm, and it felt real. Not like a dream at all.

Suddenly, someone grabbed her body and lifted her over their shoulder, and she heard a window open, followed by the sensation of falling. Her dream stopped.

CHAPTER 9

*G*avin was aroused from sleep by the smell of smoke wafting through his open window. He then heard the church bell sounding an alarm in the distance. During his years in the army and as a doctor, he had learned to sleep in a half-waking state. He threw the covers off and pulling on his shirt, breeches and boots, ran down the stairs as fast as he could, stopping only to collect his medical bag from the study. As he ran toward the stables, he could tell by the smoke and orange sky that the fire was large. It appeared to be coming from the southerly direction, and when, moments later, he saw the groom from Breconrae galloping towards him, his heart felt as if it had been ripped from his chest.

"M'lord!" the groom shouted. "Fire! Come, quick!"

Gavin turned and took the first horse from the stables, mindless of saddles, only throwing on a bridle and mounting, all the while shouting for his own grooms and stable boys to wake up and join the brigade as fast as possible.

He started out for the shortest route to the fire. The light from the moon reflecting off the billowing smoke in the sky was sufficient to guide the way. He would not later be able to recall having jumped hedges, fences or ha-has in his single-minded determination to reach Margaux.

The estate workers had already assembled in a line when he and the groom reached the Dower House. The fire was nearly put out, and the brigade was efficiently passing bucket after bucket to quench any wayward embers that might reignite. A wave of relief swept over him when he realized Margaux must be unharmed, and he quickly turned his attention to the occupants of the Dower House, who had gathered outside and were watching in disbelief and horror at the scene before them. Gavin was quickly in their midst, ensuring none of them had life-threatening injuries. He began treating those with burns and sought out Mrs. Bailey to have the sufferers moved to the manor house.

"Has anyone seen Mrs. Bailey?" Gavin asked of the girls.

Most shook their heads, but one of the older girls spoke up. "She was arguin' fierce with another lady. "Twas after she got evry 'un out the fire."

"Who was the lady?" he asked.

"Mrs. Mulligan, the vicar's wife, m'lord. But Mrs. Bailey were yellin' that she weren't s'possed to be there."

"Fire!" someone shouted. "The big house is on fire!"

Gavin turned and saw smoke rising beyond the path to the main house and ran as fast as his legs could carry him and his bag.

A corner of the manor house was ablaze, and the workers hurried behind him to assemble once more. They would be hindered by the height, though it looked to be the second storey that was alight.

"Where is she?" Gavin demanded as he looked around for his wife. Minutes before, he had thought her safe, and his mind had moved to doctoring. He fought panic, knowing it did little good. He was well trained not to panic, but never had he been so afraid. Had no one thought to wake the family? Of course! The servants were in the fire brigade.

"The family sleeps upstairs, m'lord," the groom answered, trying to catch his breath after running behind him.

Gavin covered his mouth and nose with a cloth, took a bucket from the brigade and doused himself before running into the house. He was immediately assailed with thick smoke and heat, and could scarcely see through his watering eyes. He was forced to drop to the ground and crawl when he reached the top of the stairs.

Flames were engulfing the landing with menacing heat. A large beam broke free and crashed across the doorway blocking his path. He saw a flash of clothing and tried to reach it, but was propelled backward by the force. He was too late. *Dear God, don't let it be her.* Instinct told him it was the housekeeper, but it was too difficult to see well. God rest the poor woman's soul. Sweat was pouring from him and his throat was seared. He felt as though he had swallowed a shovel of red hot coals. Despite his growing fatigue, he hastened back down the stairs and did his best to yell for a ladder and direct the men to aim water on the inside to prevent the fire from spreading.

He made his way around to the side of the house, where a group of estate workers was attempting to wet what little of the interior they could reach.

"Which window?" he gasped, trying to inhale as much good air as he could before going back in.

"There, m'lord." A servant pointed.

"You there! Follow me up in case I have need of you," he warned.

He doused himself again to relieve the heat, climbed to a window via a ladder and pushed it up before hurrying through. Underneath the frame sat Lady Ida, curled up and gasping for air. He picked up the frail woman and handed her to the servant who had climbed up behind him. But where was Margaux?

He ploughed through the door, paying little heed to his own safety. Flames were already finding their way into the next room and parts of the upper floor were caving in around him. He tried the room next to Ida's and kicked his way through the burning door. Margaux was lying asleep on the bed, flames reaching from its canopy. Smoke and flames were billowing in the room behind him as the fire began to take over the last corner of the wing.

He could feel the heat licking at his back as he wrapped her in a blanket and scooped her up into his arms. He opened the window and shouted for the men to move and catch her before he released her down to their mercy. The ladder was moved back to the window and he followed as fast as he could. Water was poured over Margaux's burns, and once he determined she was still alive, he called for his horse and carried her back to his house himself.

This was all his fault, he chastised himself, as he watched his wife struggle to breathe. If he had not sent the Mulligans away, Margaux would not be fighting for her life before him, and Mrs. Bailey would still be alive. They had not been able to find the house-mother after the fire, and he surmised it was she he had seen being engulfed when the beam fell. He assumed the woman had been trying to reach Margaux and Lady Ida, bless her soul. He had been sleeping—sleeping!—while the orphanage and manor house had been set on fire. He thought back over the day's events. He had no doubt it was deliberate, nor who was responsible. Mrs. Mulligan had been venomous, and she had been seen at Breconrae that night, arguing with Mrs. Bailey. He'd had no idea the vicar, being a man of the cloth, and his wife would be vindictive; he should have taken better precautions to protect all of them. While he had summoned several men to go after the Mulligans, it was likely they were miles away by now.

He watched Margaux as she wheezed. It would only get worse before it got better. If she could make it through the next two days, she would likely survive. But those days would not be easy. He went to the window and opened it further, hoping the cool, night air would ease the swelling in her air passages. He had tried some elixirs, but she had not swallowed much. He had set them steaming in a pot nearby, in a desperate measure to supplement what she had not swallowed. As her breathing became more high-pitched and she gasped for air, he climbed behind her on the bed to hold her in an upright position and thus give her the best possible chance. He was terrified. His skills as a physician would fail him when it mattered most. Outwardly, her burns were not too severe, but she was struggling for survival. He had seen too many cases of people dying from inhaling smoke. She had taken in much more than he or Lady Ida, who had been near the partly open window when he had found her. If he could just keep Margaux alive long enough to heal her lungs, he prayed. He felt help-less. She had to live.

He had sent one of his men express to London to inform Lord Ashbury about the marriage, the fire, and Margaux's fight for life. It would take four days, in good conditions and riding at breakneck speed, for the message to reach the capital, unless the messenger caught up with the Ashbury coach first on its journey south. He hoped he would not need to send another messenger with worse news. He had not intended to announce the marriage in such a fashion and he fervently hoped Lord Ashbury would not object —if his daughter survived. In all probability, Gavin was not the husband Margaux's parents would have chosen for their daughter, but with her recent declaration of spinsterhood, he suspected they would accept him. At least he wasn't a mere country doctor, now. Despite their force in the *ton*, they had never been high-sticklers when he had associated with them.

He had written to Lord Ashbury with as much detail as he could provide, including his suspicion that the Mulligans had deliberately set the fires. Mrs. Mulligan had been seen arguing with Mrs. Bailey. If there had only been a fire at the manor house, he might not have suspected foul play. But the Dower House had also been set alight. Thankfully, none of the girls there had suffered serious injuries. He had sent for Seamus and his apprentice from Alberfoyle, to help the injured. His attentions were centred solely on Margaux. He looked down at his wife's beautiful form, safe in his arms. He had not thought to hold her in such a way for some time to come—if ever.

He struggled to stay awake as he held her. He had also suffered some injuries in trying to rescue her and Lady Ida. The rush he had experienced was now wearing off, and he was feeling pain in places he had not realized he had been hurt. His back and arms had received only minor burns, while his throat burned and his chest was tight. But he was alive.

Lady Ida had been huddled under her window, too afraid to jump out. Tears streamed down his face as he recalled how Mrs. Bailey had met her end, trapped by a burning beam in the hallway, unable to save herself. He had nearly been too late for Margaux. She had not even wakened. A few more minutes...

"My lord?"

Gavin looked up to see the butler peering into the room.

"Master Seamus has arrived. Shall I send him in?"

Gavin nodded. Seamus would be a welcome sight, indeed.

Seamus entered the room a few minutes later. Gavin held out his hand to take his ward's. Seamus's face was sad when he looked upon Margaux. By now his son had enough training to hear her struggled breaths and know the danger for her still remained. Few words were exchanged between mentor and pupil. Words were not necessary.

"I have just come from Catriona and Maili. They told me the news. They are doing a fine job of mixing salves for the burns. I will go and assist with the orphans and Lady Ida, unless you need my help here," Seamus said, barely above a whisper.

"Nay. There is little else to do now but wait for the dropsy to pass."

"You have tried the horehound and tobacco?" Seamus asked about the combination of medicines they had learned from Lady Easton's experience with Native Indian healers in America.

"Aye. As much as I dare."

Seamus nodded and looked again at this beautiful lady in Gavin's arms struggling for breath, before turning to leave. Gavin felt powerless; the worst part of being a physician was when there was nothing more you could do but wait. Never before had the wait been so personal. He whispered encouragement to Margaux for some time, before deciding to give her another dose of medicine and allow her to rest.

"Please fight for me, Margaux. I need you to live," he mumbled in a desperate plea.

Gavin spent the longest days and nights of his life trying not to fuss over his wife. He had soon decided he much preferred the role of doctor to that of nurse. It was simpler to give remedies and check on progress the next day. Watching someone suffer, and be near helpless, was agony. As it was, he felt a fraud—an intruder. He barely knew this woman who now bore his name, yet he was seeing her in a way he was certain she would not wish.

Dawn had broken over the mountain, and crept through the break in the curtains. Seamus entered to see if Gavin was in need of anything.

"Good morning, sir. How is Lady Craig this morning?"

"Not worse, but not better."

"As is to be expected."

"Aye. How do the other patients fare?" Gavin asked.

"They are well enough. Only a few severe burns, but I expect everyone to recover fully."

"Thank you for coming," Gavin said gratefully.

"Mr. Saunders has just arrived and is tending to the young women. I thought to give you a rest."

"I doona need a break. I would like to stay until she wakens."

"Sir, shall I give you the same speech I have heard you give over and over?"

Gavin smiled. "You must take care of yourself to take care of her. It will do her no good if you also fall ill," he recited.

"Get a wash and a shave. Have some breakfast. I will come to you if she wakens—or worsens," Seamus suggested in a reassuring tone. He sounded older than his years.

"Verra well. I willna be long."

"Any change?" Gavin asked as he re-entered the room, feeling mildly refreshed from a bath, a shave, and a slice of cold meat washed down with a pot of coffee.

"She opened her eyes for a minute, but went back to sleep before I could come for you."

"That is a verra good sign, anyway. I wasna expecting her to wake for several days, considering how long she was in the fire."

"Her skin looks improved from last night."

"Yes. She no longer looks sun-poisoned. Also a positive sign."

"Is that common in a fire?" Seamus asked, eager to learn.

"Aye. I have seen the same in chimney sweeps, but the fires are no' lit when they clean. So I doona think it is from the fire, but perhaps the smoke."

"Fascinating. I wonder if anyone has reported on it. I will look in the library when I return to school," Seamus said eagerly.

Gavin could not help but gaze upon his protégé with pride. "Thank you for the reprieve. If you wouldna mind fetching some more of the horehound, I will be in need of it soon."

"Of course."

"Are her burns severe?" Seamus gestured to the bandages around her hand, neck, and part of her face.

"Some. I doona think her face will be scarred, but her hand and neck will likely be."

"'Tis a shame."

"Aye, but it willna matter if she doesna make it through tonight."

Gavin spent the rest of the day watching for any signs of worsening or improvement in Margaux. He continued to dose her and check for fever, but her breathing was still high-pitched and wheezy. That night, however, his worst fears were realized: she began to lose the fight. Her breathing slowed and grew quiet, but it was not normal. He thrust his ear next to her chest and found there was little air moving into her lungs. He only heard a faint whistle and then silence. Her skin had taken on a pale blue hue. She was dying.

He immediately rang for Seamus, and then began to perform a procedure he had only heard tell of, but had never performed. He had gone over it in his head a thousand times since he had lain Margaux on the bed, the night of the fire, fearing for this very moment. He took a deep breath, steadied the scalpel in his hand and cut a hole in her beautiful neck. Seamus handed him a small tube they had fashioned to hold her airway open.

Margaux's eyes opened immediately with pain, but her lungs filled with air. Her eyes wide with panic, she grasped at her neck as she struggled to speak.

"Shh, lass. You canna try to talk right now," Gavin spoke soothingly to her, while trying to hold the tube in place. "Doona fight. I had to place a tube in your throat. You couldna breathe."

She was trying, his brave girl; trying to solve the riddle of how to breathe without using her nose, and deal with the pain in her throat. He tried to place her back against the pillows while Seamus kept a cloth pressed to her throat to stop the bleeding. Lord, what should he do now?

Margaux was frightened, and she could not seem to speak around the tube. Had he damaged her voice? Or was it too painful from the fire?

"Seamus, please give her a small dose of laudanum." He turned his attention back to Margaux. "It will be all right, lass. Once the dropsy in your throat goes away, we can try taking the tube out."

She tried to mouth something to him. He studied her lips.

"What happened?" he asked.

She nodded slightly, clearly afraid to move her neck.

"There was a fire at the manor house and orphanage."

She tried to mouth again. *Ida.*

"Lady Ida is doing better than you. The worst of the fire was near your room."

"The servants?" she mouthed.

"Everyone will be just fine, except Mrs. Bailey. She dinna make it, lass. The orphan girls and servants are all safe."

Margaux looked perplexed, but closed her eyes. Tears rolled down her cheek, and Gavin struggled to maintain his composure. He felt his own throat tighten, and realized hers would be doing the same thing. He bent down to her ear, and began to calm her with soothing whispers until she went back to sleep.

~

Margaux felt as if she was trapped in a tunnel. It did not hurt to breathe now as much as it had, but it was strange. Air was not moving through her nose, and she could not smell. She fought to open her eyes, but it was too much effort. Where was she? Nothing seemed familiar and she felt odd. She could hear voices speaking quietly near her; was that her father? She attempted to speak, but no sound came out.

"How is she?" Margaux heard her father ask.

"She is improving now. Last night…" Gavin paused. "I had to put a tube in her throat when it was swollen shut. We almost lost her."

"Dear God." She heard her father's voice crack with suppressed emotion.

"Aye."

"Will she have that tube in her neck forever? Will she be scarred?" Lord Ashbury asked after a lengthy pause.

"I doona think so. I believe the damage in her throat will have healed enough in a few days for me to remove the tube. As for the burns, only time will tell."

"I was hoping her mother would not have to see it."

"Is Lady Ashbury returning as well?"

"Yes. I rode on horseback as fast as I could. Your man found us just south of the border. We had not made it very far with the rains. Lady Ashbury is following in the carriage."

"I am certain Margaux will be happy you are here."

"I cannot believe this has happened. I saw your note and sent for the Runners to go after the Mulligans."

"I hadna thought to do that. I sent men after them, but the vicarage was empty and the Mulligans were nowhere to be seen."

"I was surprised to hear it was the vicar. I could have sworn Iain mentioned he had dismissed him. In fact, he was going to look for a new one when next he came to town—except, of course, he died on the way."

Margaux tried to assimilate what she was hearing. Had the fire been deliberate? Had the Mulligans tried to kill her? How could someone hate her, who did not know her? Tears began to well up behind her eyes as the full realization of what had happened struck her. A strange sound gurgled in her throat and she reached for it, only to feel an object and hole where air was coming out.

"My dearest daughter?" her father asked. "You are awake!"

She nodded slightly, terrified of the pain and sensation of the object in her throat. Tears rolled down her face. She wanted to be brave, but she also wanted to panic and scream. She couldn't even do that. Her father bent over her and kissed her on the forehead.

"Hush, lass. Everything will be fine. The best thing you can do is stay calm." Her new husband's voice was very soothing as he took her hand and rubbed small circles on it.

She pointed to her throat.

"It is a tube to help you breathe."

She nodded. She remembered Gavin had told her that last night, but she had been too weary to ask more. He hadn't understood she could not talk. She tried to mouth the words. Then she made motions with her hands.

"You wish to write?" her father asked.

She nodded.

"I will find some paper and ink. You probably wish for some time alone." Gavin exited the room, and her father sat beside her on the bed.

After Gavin left, Margaux had to fight more tears. She was so thankful her father had come. She wanted to erase the past few weeks and go back to normal. She would even try to be happy in London. But none of that was possible, now that she had married.

"Are you in pain?" her father asked worriedly.

She nodded and held up her hand to indicate a little. Her father took her other hand, the one that bore her wedding ring, and fingered it gently.

"I see you decided to tie the knot behind our backs," he teased. "I only wish you had stayed at your husband's house on your wedding night."

She gave him a gentle push and narrowed her eyes in reprimand.

"Why did you do it? I have no complaints about your choice, of course, but when we left you, you were adamant about becoming a spinster or even a nun. I would have returned to walk you down the aisle, you know, though I am certain Aunt Ida did splendidly."

She had not realized it would mean so much to him.

"I am not used to one-sided conversations with four females in the house. You must think me a dead bore," he continued to jest.

She smiled.

"I will leave you to rest while I wash off the dirt of the road. But, dearest, answer me one thing. Assure me you did not marry only for our sakes?"

She had to look away. She was not prepared to answer that, even to her father. She had not expected to be questioned so soon.

"Margaux?" he asked gently.

She closed her eyes. Maybe her father would leave that question unanswered for now. She did not know the answer herself.

CHAPTER 10

*G*avin kept his distance as Lord Ashbury had taken it upon himself to sit with Margaux during the day. He visited her bedchamber to check on her progress and continue her medicines and salves, staying nearby during the night. He could not seem to overcome the feelings of guilt that encompassed him for what he had done to his wife. Did she blame him? He had overheard Lord Ashbury questioning her about their marriage and she had not answered him. Perhaps, when she was stronger, he would ask her if she wished for an annulment. Lady Ida had spoken the truth: Scottish ceremonies were not considered binding unless the marriage had been consummated.

In light of the fire, he had decided he should call off this year's solstice ball. He had enough to worry about, with his wife's injuries and overseeing the estate. The orphans were also being housed at Castle Craig until Lord Ashbury made a decision as to where he would place them. Gavin was now even more furious regarding the Mulligans' objections, having seen to the young women and their injuries. Many who were with child were little more than girls, most having been set upon by abusive masters in service. He was not about to send them back out into the world on their own. It was a difficult time, however, to have a dozen enceinte females and babies in the house, on top of all the other upheaval.

Wallace had managed to find some temporary help, until the veterans Gavin had sent for arrived from the Easton's estate. They had hired a governess, who was to start before long, so he should soon be feeling some relief. He had seen Seamus off earlier that morning, so the lad would not fall behind in his studies. As he sipped a cup of coffee, the remains of a mostly untouched breakfast before him, he decided he would spend the morning making a tour of the tenants. It would keep him from fretting over Margaux, now she seemed to be improving.

Margaux was feeling stronger and wanted to get out of bed today. She had never played the invalid well. She pushed herself up further in her bed and tentatively felt her hair. No wonder her husband barely stayed in the room. He must be shocked at her appearance. She would have to call for her maid to attend to her toilette. A bath would not go amiss either, she decided, as she was able to smell the acrid odour of smoke on her person. Was that a good sign? She had not noticed the smell before, though it must have been present.

She wiggled her toes to test her strength before becoming more adventurous and bending her knees. She would dearly like to walk to the necessary, but felt it would not be prudent. She searched for the bell-pull and tugged.

Her terrified maid entered the room, but would not look up at her. Was it as bad as that? She had left her abigail behind in London, since the woman had not wished to remove to Scotland permanently. This young village girl, whom they had hired upon arrival, had always been timid about pleasing Margaux, but what was she afraid of now? Perhaps she was not comfortable in the sick room. That was under-standable.

How could she communicate with this girl? She doubted she could read. She attempted using hand motions to point, but when the girl refused to look at her, she started trying to get out of bed without assistance. Her legs felt unsteady and she began to wobble. The girl snapped out of her fear long enough to steady her mistress. Margaux took tiny steps until she reached the bathing room. She pointed to the necessary. The maid nodded and helped her.

She was exhausted from the minor exertion, but she needed to see how horrid she looked. It had been dreadful enough to frighten the maid. It was with a great degree of thankfulness that she sank on to a stool at the dressing table.

"I will fill a bath for ye, m'lady," the maid said as she bobbed a curtsy and rushed from the room.

Margaux had never been missish. In fact, she loathed the dramatic gestures many females employed to get attention, but when she looked at herself for the first time since the fire, she did not recognize the stranger staring back at her. She gingerly fingered the tube protruding from her neck and felt sick. She felt beads of perspiration break out all over her, and the room began to spin. She was suddenly afraid to remove the dressings, but she needed to know. She would have to come to terms with her appearance. She unravelled the bandages that covered her face, arms and neck, and what she saw stunned her; she could not think. She was going to retch. She heard a knock at the door, which diverted her back to the present.

"Margaux?" It was her mother's voice.

Margaux turned to her mother, who had entered the room. When her mother looked at her and saw her wounds she let out a scream. Margaux turned toward the mirror with determination and pulled the offending tube from her neck.

Gavin had returned to the house as fast as he could when a servant found him and told him something was wrong with the ladies. A thousand scenarios played through his mind, as they were wont to do with a doctor, but he pushed them aside as he ploughed upstairs. He took the steps up to Margaux's room three at a time, where he found

Lord Ashbury bending over Lady Ashbury with a bottle of smelling salts, and Catriona pressing bandages upon Margaux's neck, while Maili was holding a cool compress to her head.

"Good God. What happened?"

He rushed to his wife's side. The tube was no longer in place but she was breathing on her own. The relief he felt was short-lived. Her bandages littered the floor and to his considerable dismay, her burns were oozing and open.

"I'm not certain," Catriona replied. "We came when we heard the screams, and found them both on the floor. Lady Margaux was holding onto her neck."

"There was blood everywhere," Maili said in a loud whisper.

He heard the rustle of skirts behind him and turned his head. Lady Ashbury had regained her senses and was sitting upright. She looked pale and worried, while her husband still hovered nearby, passing the sal volatile nervously from hand to hand.

"She pulled that thing from her neck because I screamed. I shall never forgive myself. I was shocked at her appearance," she said, clearly feeling ashamed.

"Girls, would you please show Lady Ashbury to her room, and allow me a few moments with Lady Craig?"

He took the bandage from Catriona's hand as Lord Ashbury helped his wife to her feet.

"You did well, girls." Summoning a smile from somewhere, Gavin praised his daughters.

They smiled sheepishly and followed Lord and Lady Ashbury from the room. Gavin put Margaux's hand over the bandage.

"Hold this, lass."

He scooped her up in his arms and placing her gently on the bed, sat next to her. Lifting her hand from the bandage, he eased it away from her neck to survey the damage. The bleeding had stopped and the hole was beginning to close up already. He dared to glance up at her face and saw she was watching him for his reaction.

"Are you all right, lass?"

Tears filled her brilliant, blue-green eyes and she looked away.

"If you were finding the tube uncomfortable, you only had to tell me. I would have helped," he teased. "If you ever tire of me, please warn me before you do something drastic."

She attempted to say, *I'm sorry.* It was more of a raspy, whispered sound.

"Thank goodness you were able to breathe on your own. You gave me quite a scare, there."

She looked down, as if embarrassed. He cleaned her neck gently with a cloth and placed a small bandage over the closing hole. It was a procedure he had performed hundreds, if not thousands, of times with wounds, yet it was a much more intimate process with the lady who was now his wife.

"May I examine you, now that the tube is gone?"

Margaux nodded hesitantly. Even though she knew he was a doctor, she was not just a patient to him. She likely did not want him to see her like this. She tried to take a deep breath, fighting her tears.

"What is it, lass?" he asked with concern.

She shook her head.

"Is something hurting?"

She shook her head again.

"I canna help you if I doona ken what is wrong."

She pointed to her bandaged hand and neck.

"Are you worried about the burns?"

She nodded slightly but did not look up.

"I think they will not be bad when they heal. There may be some scarring, but it should look better than it does now."

She looked up at him with those eyes he wanted to lose himself in, and she seemed to sigh with relief. He needed to keep his feelings in check. He could not risk the hurt again. He had the rest of his life with her.

"Can you open your mouth for me and try to say something?"

Her eyes widened. She put her fingers over her nose to indicate she stank. He burst out laughing.

"Verra well. I will wait until you have had a chance to wash. At least let me listen to your lungs."

She wrinkled her nose, which he found enchanting.

"Doona worry. You smell no worse than you did the first day after the fire."

She slanted her eyes at him, but he put his ear to her back before she threw him out in favour of a bath. She still had wheezes in her lungs, but she was breathing on her own. It would do for now.

"Shall I call for your maid, now?" he asked with an arched brow.

"Please," she whispered, though he could tell it was painful for her to do so.

He hoped her voice would return in time. He would miss its melodic sound, but she was alive. He hoped she saw it that way, too. It would not lessen his guilt, nevertheless.

The maid knocked on the door to tell them that Margaux's bath was ready. He noticed she did not look at Margaux—in fact, she avoided her. In an instant, Gavin had scooped Margaux up and was carrying her along the passage to the bathing room. When she realized what he was doing she held his arm and shook her head.

"Doona worry, lass. I willna look," he whispered soothingly in her ear. He was her husband, though, he thought, and had every right to. "But if you think I am going to leave you after seeing you on the floor, then you have lost your mind, wife."

He set her down on a chair near the bathtub, and directed the maid to remove her nightdress. He looked away. He would do his best to maintain her modesty. As a doctor, he had seen more unclothed body parts than he would care to recall, but he knew how he dealt with this would shadow the rest of their relationship—if they still had one when this was over.

"Now wrap a cloth around her, and I will place her in the tub."

The maid nodded and did as she was told. Gavin lifted Margaux and placed her gingerly into the water.

"You may wash her hair, but keep a cloth over her neck and hand. I will wait in the next room. Call me when you are ready."

As he turned to leave the room, he felt Margaux's hand reach out to stop him. He looked at her face, careful not to permit his eyes to drift lower.

"Thank you," she whispered.

"You are more than welcome, *mo stor*," he said tenderly.

Margaux felt very sorry for herself, and that made her angry. She told herself that she wasn't vain, that she wanted to be valued for her inward beauty, not her outward appearance. However, she had never before known what it was like to be flawed—to have people be unable to bear the sight of you. It was humiliating. She had grown accustomed to society's whispers about her outspokenness and thinking her overly particular, yet nothing approaching this repulsion. The only one who had not reacted to her appearance was her husband. He was used to seeing people with injuries. Perhaps he only pitied her, but he had been kind. It did not mean he would still want her for a wife.

She wanted to wallow in self-pity, and run home to her parents and sisters. But she had pride, and that made her dress and attempt to go down to dinner. They would have to accept her as she was now— still Margaux, only scarred. Could she accept herself?

She whispered for her maid to fetch Lord Craig. As much as she hated asking for help, she knew she could not walk down the stairs alone. She felt tired merely from the exertion of dressing. Breathing and attempting to talk were still excruciatingly painful, but she needed to prove something to herself.

She had taken extra care tonight. The girls had helped. She had found herself without clothing of her own, but her maid had been able to find some of the former Lady Craig's garments to suit. Catriona had suggested she place a ribbon around her neck, to cover where the gown did not, so Lady Ashbury would not become upset again. Margaux pondered with mixed emotions over her mother's reaction; the tube was now gone, after all. But she decided it would be best for her to appear as normal as possible. She needed to heal and carry on with her new life, and she did not know if she could with her mother unable to look at her.

There was a knock on the door, and Margaux's handsome husband stepped inside. She thought she saw a hint of appreciation in his eyes. Was it as false hope she harboured? Would he regard her so without the bandages to hide her deformities? Whether he admired her appearance or her fortitude, she dared not ask. He walked over to where she sat.

"You are beautiful, wife. Do you intend to join us for dinner?"

She looked away at the compliment. She wanted to believe him. Never before had it mattered so much. She gave a slight nod.

"May I offer you assistance?" He offered her a hand.

She wobbled and he caught her before she fell. With his arms wrapped around her, he gazed down into her eyes. Her heart was beating rapidly while she tried to catch her breath.

"Are you certain you wish to go to dinner? You have been through a great deal the past few days. I can have some dishes sent up for you, though I do not recommend anything solid yet."

She shook her head and looked to him, pleading with her eyes. "Please," she struggled to whisper. She could not stay shut away in her room.

He hesitated. "Verra well. After you take your medicine."

"Bribery!" she attempted to whisper, but when he handed her a small tumbler of elixir, she painfully swallowed the contents.

He winked, then bent down and effortlessly scooped her into his arms.

She was too shocked to try to argue.

She took the opportunity to study this new husband of hers at close quarters. He must have had ample chance to study her at her worst. If Catriona was correct, Gavin had scarcely left her side until her father arrived. He was a dutiful husband or doctor—perhaps he would have done that for any of his patients. Of course he would have.

He was inordinately handsome, but he did not seem to know it. His dark hair and blue eyes alone were enough to make her heart race, and when he smiled, the crinkles around his eyes made her forget herself entirely.

In London, any man with his looks would have the *ton* at his feet. He would no doubt be the *on dit* of the hour and be hunted by a host of high-ranking ladies, regardless of his married status. He wasn't up to snuff with fashion, of course, and did not carry himself with haughty arrogance, as was *de rigueur*, but he presented himself with calm confidence, as if he had no need to please. He would tempt the cats of society beyond bearing.

Margaux considered the realization that her husband might wish to have a presence in London. Had his brother taken his seat in Parliament? Did Gavin intend to do so? She could not contemplate London yet. Would everyone be as repulsed by her appearance as her own mother had been? Of course, they would. She had seen how injured soldiers had been ostracized. People knew in their minds that they should respect veterans and honour them for their service, but it made them uncomfortable to look at the crippled or to know what to say.

She closed her eyes as they descended the stairs and was surrounded by his scent of amber and musk. She inhaled again, deeply, wanting more, but it turned into a wheezy breath that caused her dutiful husband to look down at her with concern. How charming he must find her!

She smiled, as if begging pardon, not wishing to be caught studying him. He smiled back, and she was thankful he was holding her or she would have melted onto the floor. They reached the door of the drawing room and a footman opened it for them. She had thought he would set her on her feet, but he continued into the room to the gasps of her parents.

"Good evening. Your daughter wished to join us tonight. Would you care to follow us into the dining room?"

Margaux smiled at her parents, who were staring at her with astonishment.

"Are you certain this is wise, *chérie*?" Lady Ashbury reprimanded.

"It shouldna harm her as long as she doesna over-exert herself. As you can see, I am ensuring she doesna do that. Shall we?"

Well done, husband, she thought. It was nice to have someone else defend her for once. Gavin seated her next to him, instead of at the traditional, opposite end of the table. Most likely, he was being dutiful again. She bent her head to the soup before her, not realising how hungry she was after days with no sustenance. Swallowing was not natural. It still felt as if knives were pointing in every direction as the soup went down, and she found herself coughing indelicately and painfully. She decided to wait until later to try when she was alone. The less she appeared the invalid, the less changed they would think her.

"I rode over to survey the damage at Breconrae today." Lord Ashbury broke the painful distraction of her coughs.

"Was it a total loss? I didna go back after I found Lady Craig." Her husband referred to her.

"The servants' wing was saved. I believe we may move the girls back once we find a new house-mother."

"Perhaps Charles will wish to rebuild his inheritance," Lady Ashbury remarked. "One day, he will need a home to settle down in, since we are not planning to remove from our main house in the forseeable future."

"Do not set your hopes on it, my dear. Charles shows no indication for anything of that nature. I intend to start the rebuilding, but there need not be any hurry, since there is ample space for the girls."

"There is no need to remove them with undue haste, either. They are welcome for as long as necessary. I think my services may be needed more often than not, though Mrs. MacNair is an excellent midwife."

"That is kind of you, Lord Craig. I don't know how I would have borne it if you had not been there for Margaux," Lady Ashbury said, while delicately blotting her eyes with a lace handkerchief.

Margaux did not wish to consider what had almost happened. Where was Aunt Ida?

She reached out for Gavin's arm. "Ida?" she whispered.

"She is a stout one, Lady Ida. She is mending slowly, but as she ought."

"Your aunt is minding her doctor's orders to stay abed," Lady Ashbury remarked.

Margaux would not take the bait. She nodded. How long did her parents mean to stay? Perhaps her mother could be put to good use, if they were going to remain for the ball. She reached for Gavin's arm again.

"Yes, my lady?" He looked at her with his disconcerting eyes. He seemed amused.

"The ball," she managed to force out.

"A ball?" Her mother perked up, as Margaux had known she would.

"I was going to cancel it, lass. It is hardly the time, with your injuries and Iain's recent passing. I think the villagers will understand."

Margaux shook her head vehemently.

Gavin's eyes widened in response to her intensity.

"When is the ball to take place?" Lord Ashbury asked.

"It is our annual solstice ball. To celebrate the threshing and give to the villagers."

"That is little more than a fortnight!" her mother shrieked. "*Chérie*, we must stay until after the ball. Margaux is not yet in any condition to plan this alone." She turned to her daughter. "Not that you are not quite capable, under normal circumstances."

Margaux would not be offended. She truly did not feel up to planning a ball, and it was her mother's delight, after her children. Margaux only hoped Lady Ashbury would quell her normally grandiose tendencies. After all, this was for the villagers.

She stole a quick glance at Gavin. Smiling at her, he winked, indicating he knew she had purposely diverted her mother's attentions away from herself. She smiled coyly back at him. She wouldn't warn him *yet* about her mother's idea of throwing a ball.

CHAPTER 11

*G*avin decided he could no longer put off seeing to the estate. His wife was past danger, although her lungs would likely be weak forever. She might never regain her full voice. However, if anyone could, it was she. He chuckled as he thought of her antics the day before. She was a stubborn, clever woman!

He had wondered how someone with her beauty and wit had remained unmarried. Had she loved Lord Vernon so deeply that she could not bear to marry another? He did not wish to dwell on her past or his. She was charming, even without a voice. And her beauty went deep beyond the surface. He was surprised by her strength; when most ladies would have given up or at least stayed abed another month, she had insisted on leaving the sickroom. He had occasionally met a farmer or other labourer of her ilk, who had refused to be kept down. Margaux did not have to worry about fields or hungry mouths to feed, but she might be trying to prove something to her parents. He should keep a close eye on her and ensure she rested. She had already been going over guest lists and the menu for the ball, with her mother and Mrs. Ennis, when he had left the house. He had a sneaking suspicion that this would be the grandest ball that the county had ever seen.

He surveyed the lands from the rise. His brother had more than doubled the farmable land that his father had had. Had Iain been leasing out the farms, or had he overseen it all? Gavin had no idea. For some time, he watched over the vast estate that was now his, attempting to assimilate this new life he had inherited. A breeze swept through the ripening awns of the barley fields, rippling the crop into golden waves, and he inhaled deeply of the nostalgic scent. He felt sadness for the empire his brother had built but he would never enjoy.

It was nearing the harvest, and that meant the barley would soon be ready for malting. Gavin at least knew the barley was intended largely for whisky. Should he continue on with this venture his brother had made a substantial fortune from? Gavin had no nose for business, and not a very sophisticated one for whisky. He would have to find a use for the unfathomable amount of barley that was about to be threshed. He had honestly thought whisky to be only a hobby of his brother's. It was about to become his, he mused.

He did recognize some of the workers and greeted them while they were out tilling the land. The veterans from the Eastons' estate would be arriving soon, and he fully intended to give them useful employment. He sighed; all he wished for was to be a country doctor.

He set out from there to the old barn near the mill, to see what he was up against. His father had always enjoyed crafting whisky, but his small still had been just enough to supply the family for an entire year. Gavin was not prepared to find five giant stills that were as wide as he was tall. Good heavens! They must truly be supplying half the kingdom.

He walked around the giant tubs which currently stood waiting for the barley to finish ripening. The walls were lined with enormous oaken barrels, each labelled with their year of casking. He could not fathom what was before his gaze. This was his to undertake or it would be allowed to die with his brother. He did not wish to be involved in anything illegal. He might be heading to London more quickly than he was prepared for, if only to attempt to make this proper. Tragically, Iain had been heading to Parliament to argue for legalization when his family's carriage had gone down the side of the cliff. Meanwhile, there would be no clandestine deals for Craig whisky until he could do so with a clear conscience.

He was fairly certain he would bungle several batches before he had enough mastery over the process, as it was. He knew the family recipe was tucked away for safekeeping, but meanwhile, he hoped some of the men were wiser about Scottish moonshine than he.

"Craig? Are you in here?" Lord Ashbury's voice called to him.

"Aye." He stepped out from behind one of the rows of barrels that had been obscuring him from view.

"I had no idea," Lord Ashbury remarked appreciatively as he looked around.

"I think there is bound to be a good deal of trouble over this, if discovered," Gavin pondered with a frown.

"Or a good deal of happiness." Lord Ashbury smiled.

Gavin chuckled.

"It will be sometime before I take the operation back where Iain had it—if ever."

"You must," Ashbury insisted. "Surely this gives you an idea of how much demand there is for it."

"It doesna make it legal."

"Legal does not always mean right," Lord Ashbury protested.

"True. But I must protect my family," Gavin said thoughtfully.

"I know Iain did what was necessary to keep the estate above the hatches. It is unbelievable, the amount of upkeep these old estates require."

"Aye. It wasna always so prosperous. I doona condemn him. It was also his passion. It isna mine and I will ruin the good name of Craig if I do not take my time."

"A wise choice. It is my own pleasure that speaks more hastily than my son-in-law's," Ashbury agreed in obvious amusement.

"Doona worry. I willna let family run out. It looks like Iain left enough to keep you supplied," Gavin said, looking around at the barn stacked high with barrels.

"Only if you keep brewing at his pace," Ashbury replied, chuckling. "Once word gets out, everyone will be hounding me instead."

"I had best find someone who has experience. After I find Iain's books," Gavin said, thinking aloud.

"I am certain Easton will send the right people for you."

"Let us hope he sends some Scots. No one makes whisky like a Scot."

Lord Ashbury mumbled his agreement and began walking around to survey the monstrous stills and tubs. "How did Iain manage this alone? I cannot imagine."

"I suspect once it is started, it is largely watching and waiting. I heard Father tell once of placing it all in the still and allowing magic to happen." Gavin's face took on a look of deep consternation. He lifted the lid on one of the large pots and the strong aroma of a barley field accosted him.

"It doesna smell like whisky. 'Tis more like beer," he said, surprised.

"That must be where the barley malts and concentrates before it is placed in the still. After you place it in the still, the whisky forms," Lord Ashbury remarked.

"We will be harvesting the barley soon. I have until then to learn."

"I suppose it is time to find your brother's books," Lord Ashbury suggested.

"Aye. I suppose it is."

~

Margaux listened to her mother giving instructions to the cook and the housekeeper, interspersed with frequent exclamations. "La! I know not how we will manage anything approaching a decent ball!" she declared with Gallic gestures of her hands. "There is no time to send to London for anything!"

"We doona need anythin' so fancy," Mrs. Ennis dared to protest once, but she was given a quelling look by Lady Ashbury.

"My daughter will also be presented as Lady Craig. I want it to be *parfait.*"

After that, Mrs. Ennis sniffed in occasional disparagement and muttered darkly that anything Glasgow had was as fine as could be found in London.

Margaux suppressed a smile and did not bother to protest. In the past two-and-twenty years, she had learned it was useless.

She decided her time would be better served elsewhere, and that she would like to tour the castle and become more acquainted with her new home. She would prefer to explore rather than sit here.

She stood up; at once, her mother ceased the list of instructions and directed her attention.

Margaux held up her hand and whispered. "Do not trouble yourself, *Maman*. I am only going to the parlour." She shook away the offer of assistance. It was time to prove she was made of sturdier stuff—to her mother and herself. She knew she was not ready for stairs, but surely she could manage a room or two. She had never been beyond the first floor, except for her new bedroom—a chamber which adjoined her new husband's, she had noticed for the first time last night. He had brought her back there and walked through it to her own after kissing her on the cheek and whispering to her in Gaelic again. Sometime soon, she would gather the courage to ask him what he was saying. She was not quite ready to know.

She walked upright as normally as she could for her mother's benefit and sought the nearest chair as soon as she was beyond the door. Her wheezing sounded loud enough for the entire castle to hear. Once her breathing had settled, she looked at the room about her and felt a pang of guilt. She had entered a private study. Even her kind and loving father did not allow his children into his private study without permission. She could not help but be curious about her new husband, and there was something about a man and his sanctuary that drew her to it.

She had never met anyone quite like Gavin. No man had ever been so kind or gentle with her. Men of society were, of course, never allowed the intimate liberties—unless they were doctors. She blushed when she thought of how Gavin had respected her privacy in the bathing room, although he had likely wanted to laugh. Perhaps his experience as a doctor explained much of it. But Sir Henry, the doctor her family occasionally employed in London, was not particularly kind or gentle. He was direct and to the point.

She looked about her from a comfortably worn leather chair. It must have been a favourite chair for generations. There was another like it flanking the opposite side of the fireplace. On the small table next to her, an old pipe sat beside an open book of poetry. Did her husband smoke? She had never noticed the smell about him. Perhaps the pipe had been his brother's.

The room was not large. An over-sized desk occupied the far side of the room, and it was piled with papers. The far wall held obviously well-loved books. It was a comfortable room. She wanted one for herself. Perhaps there was such a room for her. She would have to ask.

Her eyes were drawn to the portrait above the mantle.

A handsome couple, surrounded by three healthy-looking, blue-eyed boys, looked down upon her. The man looked very like her husband. *Iain*. He even had the same eyes, with laughter lines surrounding them. He was looking at his wife with adoration. Margaux felt a stab of jealousy. She wanted to be looked at like that. Iain obviously had been in love with his wife. Love did not happen when you married for convenience.

The late Lady Craig had been a red-headed beauty, but her eyes were not so welcoming. She was likely wondering why this stranger was in their home trying to take her place, Margaux thought. Why was she here? Why had she gone against her own principles and married for convenience? She did not belong in this home where love was synonymous with marriage. She had taken that away from Gavin and herself.

A few tears escaped and trickled down her cheek. She was feeling sorry for herself again and should go to her room, her inner voice chastised, but she was too fagged to climb the stairs. She sank into the chair and dared to put her feet upon the accompanying footstool and made herself comfortable. She only needed a few minutes to rest and then perhaps she would be able to go a little farther.

~

Gavin entered his study with the express purpose of finding Iain's journals. Iain had once mentioned he kept them under lock and key, and Gavin assumed he would have placed them in the vault. When he walked in and saw his wife sleeping in the chair, he motioned to Lord Ashbury, who smiled and crept back out of the room, closing the door behind him.

Gavin looked at his lovely wife, who was audibly wheezing, and shook his head. He felt a wave of protectiveness come over him. One day, he hoped they would mutually feel more than that. He did not want her to feel trapped or to resent him. Why was she in his study? Had she been waiting for him? He watched her for a while, before turning his attention back to finding the journals. He opened the vault as quietly as he could and searched through decades of deeds, wills, and other official-looking papers. Nothing resembled a whisky recipe. He did find several cases of family jewellery, and he realized he should have presented them to his wife. To be fair, he hadn't really had an opportunity. He had given Margaux the family ring, because it had been passed to him before Iain's wife was buried. He would give Margaux these other jewels before the ball. She might not be able to dance, but she would look the part of Lady Craig. Although, he mused, glancing at his wife with a rueful smile, the stubborn woman would no doubt try to dance.

He placed everything back into the vault as he had found it, then sat in the chair opposite Margaux to think. Mayhap Iain had another safe place somewhere in the house—perhaps in his apartment. For a moment, he toyed with looking in their hiding places from childhood, but it was whisky recipes he was seeking, he reflected, not a treasure chest.

He gazed over at his wife, and to his surprise, she was watching him. He smiled.

"Guid day."

"Good day," she whispered and blushed.

"Are you feeling ill?"

She shook her head. "I was tired," she rasped.

"I am glad you rested, then. Would no one help you to your room?"

Her cheeks flushed. "I was alone. I was exploring, but only got this far. I'm sorry."

"Doona be sorry. Everything I have is yours. No secrets. No forbidden rooms. Now, doona try to talk so much. Your voice needs to heal."

She nodded, but was still embarrassed.

"Is something missing?" She indicated the vault he had been searching through.

"I can see I will need to fashion a writing case for you to keep with you." He smiled and moved to sit on the stool next to her feet. "I am looking for my brother's whisky journals. I was about to see if he kept them in our apartment. Would you like me to take you upstairs?"

She flushed again. Lord above, she was beautiful. He hadn't meant it the way she was thinking. Would it be worse if he corrected himself? She was staring at him with those beautifully innocent eyes. The burns did not diminish her beauty in the least. She wasn't answering him, and they were staring at each other. It dawned on him: she was waiting for him to give her paper.

"Now you are being a little minx. You could nod your head to that question."

She looked coy and he laughed. He made the decision for her and scooped her into his arms. He rather liked holding her. He suspected this independent woman would never have allowed him this close were she not so severely hurt.

She leaned her head against him, and he decided it was one of the greatest feelings. His life had been happy, and Seamus and the girls looked up to him, but she was putting her trust in him as her husband. Even if they had no more than friendship in this marriage, he would cherish that gift.

CHAPTER 12

*G*avin placed Margaux on a chair in their private sitting room. "Any ideas for hiding places?" he asked. Lacking an alternative, ladylike gesture, she shrugged her shoulders in response as he scanned the room between their apartments. It was a room Margaux approved of. It was neither masculine nor feminine, decorated in cool tones of blue that were soothing. It was a room she could spend hours in, cosily reading or doing household accounts. It only wanted books.

She looked for a place a vault might be hiding, but there was nowhere obvious. She stood and went to the small writing desk, but no journals were hiding inside. There were miniatures of Iain's children sitting atop the smooth mahogany surface, and she once again felt an intruder in a place where she did not belong. Would she ever feel rightfully Lady Craig?

She cast away her thoughts and continued to look about. There was a landscape above the mantel, but nothing hiding behind. Gavin had wandered into his room and Margaux hesitated at the threshold, debating if she should enter too. She stood and watched this relative stranger, and realized nothing was different about marriage thus far other than her name, but she wanted to know this man.

She could not imagine any other man of her acquaintance treating her with the kindness he had shown her, yet not treating her differently after the fire. She did not know how she would appear when she healed, but she could not imagine it would be beautiful. Perhaps he did only wish her to run his home and offered her the protection of his name in exchange. It was what they had agreed to, but it somehow left her feeling empty.

"I doona think they are here, either."

He turned to look at her and smiled kindly when he caught her staring at him. "You look tired, lass."

He walked toward her and tucked her arm in his and led her to a chair. She shook her head and began to pull the pen and paper out of the desk to write.

I am not tired. She underlined 'not' for emphasis.

He laughed. "Verra well, not tired. I am gonna look in some of our old hiding places. Would you care to join me?"

She began writing furiously.

Margaux will join you.

"Margaux, would you care to join me?" he asked gallantly.

She smiled and nodded her head.

He bent over and picked her up before she could think about standing on her own. Her face must have shown the shock. She wanted to write, but he was jostling her too much as they bounced up a staircase.

"I willna carry you for the rest of our lives, but we are going too far right now. I suggest you accustom yourself to it, or I will order you back to your bed despite your terms. Doctor's orders overrule your husband's."

She wrinkled her face and pulled the skin where she had been burned. She let out a squeak. He looked at her, but seemed satisfied she was unharmed and kept going up a circular staircase. They must be going to one of the towers she had seen at the front of the house. He set her down before a door.

"Iain and I used to play here for hours," he said fondly.

The door opened and the round room was littered with a collection of boyish items. He chuckled and picked up one of the hundreds of arrows that were scattered about the room. The ends of the arrows had been covered with a ball and fabric, likely to soften the blow of an errant shot.

He picked up a bow and some of the practice arrows and walked to one of the slitted windows. He removed the covering and took aim. She could not help but admire the strength with which he held the bow and pulled the string with ease. Margaux wondered what he was shooting towards and walked over to look. He turned and noticed her curiosity.

"Forgive me for becoming distracted. The old target is still there and I couldna resist," he said with a smile.

She held out her uninjured hand for the bow.

"It will hurt your hand," he protested.

She shrugged but took the bow. She had practiced for hours with her brother, Charles, when he was learning. She pulled back the bow and was afraid she would not be able to muster the strength, but her pride urged her on. The pain in her hand was excruciating, yet she made a credible shot before grimacing and dropping the bow.

Gavin whistled appreciation.

"Verra nice shot, milady." He bowed. "When you are healed properly, you may challenge me. But as your doctor, I insist no more for now."

She nodded. She did not wish to repeat the pain. They continued to survey the room, including Gavin removing a stone from the floor to reveal a hiding spot underneath. There was no more than a boys' treasure-trove of rocks, sticks and a few toys. Gavin looked mildly amused and disappointed.

"I didna really expect them to be there, but I doona ken where else to look."

She pulled the ink, paper and quill from her pockets and found a small table to write on.

Where did he distil the whisky?

"At one of the barns. I didna see anythin' there."

She frowned with disappointment.

"But I didna look verra hard. I assumed the books would be in the vault in his study."

Try again? She wrote eagerly.

"Verra well. I suppose you wish to join me?"

She smiled sheepishly. She was scooped off her feet before she could nod.

Gavin did not carry her the entire way, but placed her next to him in the small one-horse gig he had called for earlier. It was the first time she had watched him handle the reins, and the first time she had gone beyond the front drive of the property. She had no idea what lay past the wooded park surrounding the house. They came upon the fell, and a breathtaking view of a valley covered in amber-coloured grains and hedgerows, surrounding the eastern side of the property as far as her eyes could see. The western edge sloped down into the loch and was dotted with grazing sheep. She remembered why she had chosen Scotland. She inhaled deeply with appreciation, causing her husband to glance at her.

She smiled and mouthed, "It is lovely."

"Aye, that it is. Our property extends farther than we can see to the north and east. Your father's property borders ours on the south, and the western border goes to the Firth."

He urged the horse forward and they reached a large barn near the loch.

"Shall we?"

Gavin reached up and circled her waist with his large hands, and a simultaneous pulse of awareness and depression came over her. She could not deny the attraction she felt for this man who only wanted a lifelong partner. It could be much worse, she reminded herself.

They entered the multi-storeyed barn. Margaux could not recall ever having been in any such place. A strange smell scented the building—perhaps that of grain. There were giant casks and tubs with pipes and oars for stirring.

Margaux's curiosity took hold and she attempted to stir one of the oars around a large tub of water. It was surprisingly difficult. She caught her husband watching her with amusement. She shrugged.

"I imagine when the barley is added, it will be nigh impossible for you to stir," he challenged.

She pulled a mischievous face and mouthed, "We shall see."

He laughed and she began searching for the mysterious journals. She found a small room at the back of the barn, and he followed her inside.

"They aren't here either," he said with great disappointment.

She tried to think. Did his brother do all of this work on his own? It seemed too much for one person. Would her husband not have asked the necessary people?

She gratefully sunk into a nearby chair and once again scribbled on her paper, thankful there was a pot of ink in which to dip her quill. *Who helped him? Can you ask them?*

Gavin looked at her blankly.

"I doona ken. I assumed he did everathin' but I suppose Wallace might have some idea."

She nodded her head, though she was inwardly shaking it. Men could be daft sometimes.

"I will ask him tomorrow. I think you have had enough adventure for today."

She did not want to be done. She had not enjoyed a day more as long as she could remember. But she was tired.

"I will take you to rest before dinner."

She gave him a mildly conciliatory look.

"You speak a thousand words without speaking, dear wife."

She eyed him as if to say, *Oh?*

He laughed at her.

"And that was one of those comments I would have been better to keep to myself."

Still chuckling, he pulled her into a side hug and kissed the top of her head—exactly as he would have done to a sister.

∾

Catriona was enjoying her new-found importance. Mr. Saunders had allowed the girls to help him as he attended to the burns of the orphans, and Catriona especially had taken an interest in learning about herbs and their healing properties. She had taken it upon herself to search for the herbs that were not already grown by Lord Craig and prepare the salves. Some of the recipes she had been given by Lady Easton, who had, to an extent, studied medicine while living in America.

One recipe in particular had caught her eye, and she thought Lady Margaux might wish to try it. They had already been treating her burns with a salve and they were improving, but Lady Easton's notes made it sound miraculous. Catriona hoped this would restore the porcelain skin that was still blistered and raw.

She searched high and low for the ingredients, including asking Mrs. Ennis to send to Glasgow for those she could not find, and had finally, hopefully, come close to the right mixture after trying for days. She sought out Lady Margaux and knocked on the door of her room.

"Good day, Lady Craig," Catriona said as she made a curtsy.

"Good day," Lady Margaux whispered back. She was sitting at her dressing table, brushing her hair. The maid was nowhere in sight.

"I have come to dress your wounds. I have a new salve I have prepared that I would like to try."

Lady Margaux looked up at her sceptically.

"Do not worry. It is one of Lady Easton's recipes, and Lord Craig said I may try it. Her notes made it sound miraculous."

Lady Margaux's face fell a little.

"Forgive me. I should not say such things. You are still very beautiful. I only thought how nice it would be for you not to have scars or pain."

Lady Margaux reached up and brushed the side of Catriona's face lovingly. She stood and walked over to the chaise lounge and motioned for Catriona to join her, wheezing with the simple exertion. She held out her wounded arm for the girl's ministrations.

Catriona felt Lady Margaux cringe as she removed the bandages. It was hard to find anything that did not stick to the open skin. Mr.

Saunders had told her to use very thick amounts of salve so it would not hurt. Lady Margaux would not look at the burns after that dreadful day her mother had screamed at her appearance. She had looked a fright, to be sure, but she was still one of the most beautiful people Catriona had ever seen. She admired Lady Margaux's courage in acting as though nothing was different about her.

The only strange thing Catriona had found was Lady Margaux preferred her to dress her wounds instead of Lord Craig. Catriona didn't mind. She was flattered, actually. Lady Margaux's maid would scarcely look at her, so Catriona had been helping her dress and style her hair when she asked. Maili loved to brush her long ebony hair until it shone like silk. Lady Margaux did not seem to be affected by Maili's exuberance.

When Catriona had the dressings removed, she took the water basin and began to wash the dead skin away with a cloth, as she had been told. Lady Margaux winced a few times, but was strong as always. Catriona was about to burst with excitement at trying the new salve. Lady Margaux was sniffing at the new mixture.

"What is it?" she rasped.

"Mostly honey, wormwood, marshmallow root, comfrey root, white oak bark, lobelia, and a strange plant Lord Craig grows in the conservatory called aloe vera. He said Lady Easton gave him the plant, which she brought back from America."

Lady Margaux shrugged. Catriona applied a thick layer of the cream and Lady Margaux let out a sigh.

"Does it feel nice?"

Lady Margaux nodded. "It doesn't sting."

Catriona was pleased. The new salve already showed promise, but would it keep Lady Margaux from scarring?

She tenderly covered the burns on Lady Margaux's neck and cheek and then re-bandaged them with cloths.

"Shall I help you dress for dinner?"

Lady Margaux shook her head and touched her arm.

"Thank you."

Catriona smiled and went on her way to mix some more of the salve.

~

Margaux watched Catriona close the door, then wept with hopelessness and acceptance. She had dared to look at the burns for the first time since the episode with her mother. They did not look better. The skin did not hurt as much as it had and was no longer raw, but it was tight, puckering and itched horribly. Her face appeared to have escaped the worst. She must have instinctively held up her hands to protect it. But her neck and hand would never look as they had. There was a scar in the centre of her neck from the tube, and half of it also looked like the skinned animal carcasses she had seen hanging in front of butchers' shops. She couldn't abide looking at it. She couldn't blame people for not wanting to look at her either.

She struggled inwardly. She knew with all of her heart that outward appearance was not what mattered, but no longer having flawless beauty, she had to fight her desire to cower away and hide. She knew she had to keep facing the world to convince herself she mattered.

Her husband treated her the same as he had before. Was that all she was ever to know? She had hoped before the fire that there might, one day, be affection between them. She could not blame him. His heart had not been attached, and he seemed to be merrily attending to business as usual. She needed to do the same. It was what she had asked for, after all, but somehow she wanted more and had no right to expect it.

CHAPTER 13

The next morning, Gavin found Wallace sorting through piles of correspondence.

"Guid morning, Wallace. I didna expect to see you here so early."

"That arnica tea you recommended has made me bones feel better. Ye might have me for a few more years yet, lad."

"You can stay as long as you wish, Wallace. Say, would you happen to ken where Iain's journals were kept? I canna find them anywhere."

"Aye. A few months before the accident, there was a fire in the barn, so he moved them to the dungeon where yer da used to work. The old still is down there, and he would try new things out before making a grand batch."

Gavin sighed audibly. "I didna ken there was a fire in the barn. I shoulda thought of the dungeon. Thank you, Wallace."

"Aye, m'lord."

Gavin began to hurry down to the old dungeon stairs, but thought better of it and returned back up to get Margaux. He smiled when he thought of her interest in helping him. She was likely bored to tears, and this was something small he could do for her. He knocked, but did not hear a response. Of course. She couldn't talk loud enough yet.

He cracked open the door and her beautiful eyes stared back at him with amusement.

"Guid morning, lass," he said more huskily than was seemly. He needed to control his reaction to her, but the more time he spent with her, the more he feared he was losing that battle. She opened the door to let him in somewhat shyly, and he saw that her hair had not been dressed and half of the buttons on the back of her gown were open.

"Where is your maid, lass?"

She sighed, but turned to face him.

"She is afraid of me," she whispered, then turned her back, likely to hide tears.

"We will find you a new maid, lass," he whispered and began to fasten her buttons. He felt his hands trembling and took a deep breath. He hoped she could not feel his reaction to her, or she would shy away. She shivered at his touch, and he pulled away as soon as he had finished.

"I could attempt to dress your hair," he teased.

She shook her head and walked to the dressing table. With deft hands, she quickly managed to somehow pull her cascades of black silk into a loose knot—quite impressive, considering one of her hands was bandaged. She turned and looked at him expectantly. She must be wondering why he was gaping at her in her room. He cleared his throat.

"Wallace said Iain kept his books in the dungeon. I thought you might wanna come with me to look."

"Yes," she whispered with a glorious smile.

"Have you broken your fast?" he asked, glancing toward a cup of chocolate sitting by the bedside.

She nodded.

"More than a cup of chocolate? You must eat to heal properly, lass."

She looked guilty.

"Does it hurt you? To swallow?"

"A little," she confessed with a raspy voice.

He walked over toward her and placed his hands on her throat gently and felt around.

"Swallow for me, lass," he directed, and felt her neck as she did so. "Everything feels normal, but it takes time to heal on the inside."

She tugged his hand and began to pull him toward the door. He laughed.

"Not so fast." He hurried up behind her and playfully swept her off her feet. "It is a long way to the dungeon," he explained. How else was he to be close to her?

He inhaled the smell of lavender and some other mystery scent he could not identify, but which he associated with her. She leant her head against his shoulder as he carried her down the separate flights of stairs. The first was covered in a luxurious carpet. The second was wooden and bare in the servants' stairway, and when they reached the heavy wooden door to the dungeon, he set her down in order to unlock it. It was positively medieval.

Gavin had not been in the dungeon since he was a boy. It was silly how he still became excited and nervous at the same time. He knew there were no ghosts or prisoners awaiting him, yet he could not escape the memories of hunting for them and screaming with fright as he and Iain had done as boys.

The door opened and the stone stairs appeared slick as he held up the lantern to light the path. He hesitated about carrying Margaux.

She squeezed his arm from behind as she leaned forward and saw the stairs.

"I'll walk. I can, you know," she teased, even through her whispers.

"Verra well, but you must hold on to me."

They crept slowly down the musty stairs and Gavin led them to a room which looked similar to the barn, but on a much smaller scale. He set the lantern down and looked around. It was very much the same as it had looked when his father had been alive.

Margaux was also looking around and was waving him over to the work bench. There sat one of the leather-bound journals his father had used, and then Iain. He fingered it gingerly, and looked through the pages. His brother had added considerable notes and there were several recipes, which he had labelled with names.

"It looks as though Iain had a number of different recipes. I have my work cut out for me."

"I can help." His beautiful wife looked at him with those large, enchanting eyes of hers.

"Be certain you mean that, lass. I will need all the help I can find. We are to have several hundred tons of barley at our disposal in a matter of days."

"Then we best start."

She turned to head back to the passageway, but stopped as she found several smaller barrels labelled as Iain's recipes.

She looked at him with curiosity.

"We should taste them."

"Aye. I didna ken you had a taste for whisky."

"I don't know if I do or not. But I may as well start now if I am to be of any help."

"Your father should be here for this," he decided.

She nodded her agreement.

"Let us find him and we may bring the samples upstairs to a better room," Gavin suggested. He did not wish to point out that her breathing had become more laboured and wheezy in the damp cold of the basement.

He held out his arm to escort her, and she snuggled close so they could climb the narrow stairs together. She was struggling by the time they reached the wooden door, and Gavin scooped her up and transported her to the luxury of the parlour, where her mother was in counsel with the housekeeper.

Gavin bowed to the ladies.

"Would you happen to ken where Lord Ashbury is, *madame?*" he asked.

"*Oui.* He only came in from his ride a few moments ago. He is changing upstairs."

"Verra good. I will return shortly with the samples." He winked at his wife before bowing himself out of the room.

~

Margaux's mother raised an enquiring eyebrow at her and she had to fight a blush. She had largely been avoiding her mother, not wanting to experience again the humiliation she had felt when her mother had screamed at her appearance. She didn't blame her *maman*, but she felt her parent ought to be able to control her emotions around one's children. She was disappointed in her mother, though she knew she loved her—perfect or not.

"*Bonjour, chérie.*" Her mother sauntered across the room to kiss her cheek.

"*Bonjour, Maman,*" Margaux rasped.

Her cheek was healing, but she still covered it so no one would have to see it. She had taken care to cover her neck and hand at all times, too, but she could still hear the screams.

"You are enjoying your husband, *non?*" her mother asked innocently.

What did she mean by enjoying him?

"I suppose so. He is very kind," she whispered.

"There is a *modiste* to arrive soon from Glasgow. She is not Madame Monique, but we will have to make do."

"I do not need a new gown. Lady Craig left beautiful gowns and we are of a size," Margaux protested, though it pained her to do so.

"I will not argue, Margaux. You must have a proper gown for your first appearance as Lady Craig."

"But I cannot dance!" she squeaked.

"Do not try to argue, *chérie,*" her mother said more softly. "It is hurting your voice. Allow me only one dress, please."

Margaux did not like to be made to feel guilty, but her mother would be gone soon, and she would miss the badgering.

Her father entered the room with her handsome husband. She could watch Gavin all day, she realized. His eyes, his dark hair, his dimpled smile, the lilt in his voice…

He cleared his voice. He had caught her staring. She blushed, but smiled directly at him.

"I asked if you want to try them all?" He held out his hand to indicate four decanters he had brought from the casks in the dungeon.

She nodded, but held up pinched fingers to indicate only a small amount. Her mother stared at her with open shock. Her husband placed four small tumblers of amber-coloured liquid in front of her, and he and her father joined her with their samples, looking amused.

Her father took over the proceedings. Gavin had brought a quill and paper and began to take notes.

"Notice the colours are all different," Lord Ashbury instructed.

Gavin nodded and wrote something.

"Next, smell the different aromas."

They all lifted each one.

"This one is especially peaty," her father remarked as he swirled the liquid and wafted it under his nose, though Margaux had no notion of what peat actually smelled like, or why he was making strange movements with the glass.

"Smell the smoke in this one."

"Do I detect orange in this?" Gavin asked curiously.

She was clearly out of her depth. All she could smell were strong spirits, and they burned her nose. She would blame the fire for damaging her sense of smell. She remained quiet and tried to learn.

"None of these are the signature Craig whisky I have been receiving from Iain," her father remarked.

"He must have been trying to make something new."

"Shall we taste?" her father asked, with unrestrained excitement.

"Aye." Gavin set down his quill. "First, the one marked Lomond."

Margaux's father took a small sip. Her husband followed. She did the same.

Fire and burning. She could not take it! She swallowed some, some went up her nose, and the rest of the tumbler spilled on her arm, causing her to yelp with pain.

Her husband was instantly at her side, tearing the bandages off her arm and yelling for water. She tried to protest, but there were suddenly people everywhere, trying to help, and all witnessing her shame—including the *modiste* who had arrived and stood there staring at her charred arm with disgust.

She could not even speak loudly enough to ask everyone to leave.

Her husband was rinsing the offensive whisky from her arm and she began to shake with sobs.

When Gavin saw she was crying, he immediately carried her away from the madness. He felt like an idiot. Why had he not realized how the whisky would feel to her raw throat? He had been so enthralled with her eagerness to help him and learn, that he had not been thinking. When everyone had gathered around her and he had attended to her burns, they had sat there gawking. The servants, her family, the *modiste*. No wonder she had not been letting him attend to her dressings. She was ashamed—and very private. She had been courageous to continue showing her face and trying to learn the estate.

Gavin was, of course, used to seeing wounds. But he still found her beautiful—breathtakingly so; and the more time he spent with his wife, the more he found himself wanting to know more about her. He placed her on the chaise longue in her room and looked into her eyes.

"Are you all right, lass?"

She looked up at him with a glassy stare, but nodded.

"I need to look at your arm."

She held it out for his inspection, but looked away, obviously not wanting to see his reaction. He could not blame her after the response she had received downstairs. The arm was healing better than he had expected. Her hand was the most severely injured, and the arm was still pink with denuded skin.

"It looks verra good."

She looked at him with incredulity. He saw a spark of anger in her eyes, yet she said nothing.

"I think the arm will not scar too much. The hand, you must start to move more or it will become too stiff."

She cocked her head with question. He took her hand and began to massage it. She winced in pain, but allowed him to continue.

"We need to do this at least morning and night to keep it from becoming permanently tight."

Her eyes looked at him with fear. He pulled her into a loving hug. How could he make her understand? He held her for a few minutes and stroked her hair. He could offer meaningless words of encouragement, but he did not think she would appreciate it. All he could do was try to understand how she felt and be there for her.

He reluctantly pulled away and smiled at her.

"It is early yet. I doona think it will look like this forever. If it does, we will keep it covered when we go in public."

He reapplied salve, placed another bandage atop and smiled at her as he stood.

"Shall I send the *modiste* to you?"

She shook her head vehemently.

"Would you prefer your mother?" he asked, mildly jesting.

Her eyes grew round. She was contemplating.

"I suppose. I will not see the *modiste*."

"Verra well." He could not blame her.

CHAPTER 14

*I*t was some time before her mother came to her. Margaux had stayed in her room, pondering her future. She could not hide away forever. She would surely go mad. They could not send everyone away who was frightened by her appearance. Or could they? The thought amused her as much as it saddened her.

"*Chérie.*" She heard her mother's voice.

She looked up to see Lady Ashbury looking in on her. Margaux looked behind, hoping she was not going to force the seamstress upon her.

"I sent the *modiste* away. I gave her your measurements and asked her to create something to hide your injuries. I also ordered several dresses for Catriona and Maili."

Margaux was too tired to protest. She nodded instead. She was mostly relieved she would not have to face the *modiste* who was frightened of her. Why could people not see beyond the injuries? She was the same person she had been before.

"I believe everything is set for the ball. Your father and I will be returning to London the next morning, if you are agreeable. We have secured a new house-mother, who will be arriving with the veterans from Easton. We expect them on the morrow. We should see everyone settled at Breconrae by the time we depart."

Margaux nodded. She felt guilty at her relief on hearing the announcement. She needed privacy to heal. She was holding out a small fraction of hope that she would not be marred forever.

"*Merci, Maman,*" she whispered.

Her mother took her uninjured hand.

"Are you happy, *chérie*? Gavin has told us that the marriage can be annulled if you wish for it."

Margaux could not describe the sense of anguish that filled her heart at hearing those words. Did Gavin wish to be free of her now? She knew she had married without love, but she had thought their relationship had promise. But still, she had no wish for an annulment. She had been happier in her short time as Lady Craig than she had the entirety of her time as a single miss in London.

"*Oui, Maman.*"

She would discuss the annulment with her husband, but she would not with her mother. If he wished to be free, then she would grant him that for everything he had given her. It was the very least she owed him, not to mention her life. Margaux did not think her parents would argue this time about giving her her freedom. She would not leave without a fight, however. She would fulfil her end of the agreement with Lord Craig, and if he wished for her to go, then she would depart knowing she had done her best. She would also be leaving her heart behind.

Margaux set out to complete her tasks. She was breathing better and had more energy than she had, even yesterday, but she was determined to be the wife Gavin needed. She had no time for being an invalid. As she surveyed the running of things, she found Mrs. Ennis directed the household without a hitch—she brought Margaux the menus for courtesy approval, the linens were superb, each maid knew her duties and performed them admirably—save hers—she thought unkindly, and tried to erase the thought. Even the bookkeeping was in perfect order.

She was little help with the girls, though she did allow Catriona to minister to her wounds and Maili to brush her hair. Her mother was working on their French with them, and Aunt Ida was teaching them some piano. Aunt Ida had not been as affected by the fire as had Margaux, thankfully. She likely would not have survived, at her age.

Margaux passed by the drawing room and saw the baskets were prepared, ready to be filled with gifts for the tenants. The tables and chairs were in place, with crisp linens for the supper. She next sought out the ballroom, where the floor had already been polished to a high shine and fresh candles were waiting. It was too soon for the flowers. She fought her fatigue. There appeared to be nothing whatsoever for her to do. She was not actually needed, as Gavin had thought. Perhaps when her mother left there would be something, she tried to remind herself. In the meantime, she should try to help her husband with the whisky.

She took a deep breath and forced herself to walk to his study, but he was nowhere to be found. Wallace, the old steward who had married them, looked up at her.

"Guid day, milady," his thick brogue greeted her.

"Hello, Wallace. Would you happen to know where Lord Craig is?"

"Aye. He is down seeing to the barley. Left sprouting, 'twas. He is trying to see if it is salvageable."

That did not sound good at all to Margaux.

"Thank you."

She had not the energy to walk to the barn, so she asked Tallach to have the gig brought around for her. The horse was old and accustomed to making its way to the barn. She did little driving and was grateful. If the horse had been lively, she would not have been able to cope with her hand bandaged.

The horse began slowing without being checked when it reached the barn. Margaux climbed down and left the gig where it was. She was certain it would not wander far.

She entered the barn and her cheeks flushed at the heat. It was painfully warm in there. She was wearing more clothing than was normal for the summer, but the late Lady Craig's gowns had high necks, long sleeves, and were made of fabrics suited to winter—and to covering her wounds.

The kilns were fired for roasting the grain, and several men, all shirtless and dripping with sweat, were loading it into them. Margaux tried not to stare at them, and their bodies that were so different from her own: hard, muscular, and many were covered with hair almost like fur. When she saw her husband was one of the loaders, she could not take her eyes from him. He looked like a statue come to life. Her heart began racing and she realized her feelings must be written on her face. She turned away and wondered if she could sneak off before they saw her, but Gavin looked up as she began to back away.

"Margaux?" he asked with concern. He walked toward her with no self-consciousness at his state of undress. She wanted to reach out and see if his skin felt like hers. She didn't think it would. She stopped herself before doing such a thing. He would be horrified if he knew her thoughts.

"Margaux?" he asked again. His eyes were twinkling when she looked up.

Her face was on fire, from the heat and embarrassment. She needed to find a way out of there. It was becoming difficult to breathe. Gavin's expression changed and she found herself in his sweaty arms. She placed her head and hand on his chest as he led her outside. His skin definitely felt different from hers, but she was too dizzy to notice more than that.

"Lass?"

She heard him say it to her and she tried to concentrate. He began unbuttoning her gown to help her cool off.

She shook her head and tried to fight him.

"No," she protested.

"I need to cool you down. I willna let anybody see."

He set her down in the gig and moved it behind the building. He returned to the barn and came back with a bucket and his clothing. He walked over to the loch and filled the bucket, and then dipped a handkerchief into it and began bathing the back of her neck and forehead.

"Is that better?"

She nodded. She did feel better, and extremely embarrassed. Instead of showing him how capable she was, she had only shown him the opposite. She had to fight tears. When she had cooled down, he re-buttoned her gown.

"Did you need something?"

She at least should explain why she had been so bold as to venture out here on her own.

"I wanted to help," she said breathlessly.

"I thank you for that. I ken you want to help, and I will let you do so when you are healed. It is hot as Hades in there, however, and it isna good for your breathing."

"I'm sorry." A lone tear escaped and he reached up to wipe it away.

"Doona be sorry. I am only sorry you are suffering. Besides, I canna let you compare me to all the burly lads in there, or you will think your husband is puny." He laughed.

"No," she whispered and reached out to touch his chiselled chest. He shivered in response and took her hand and brought it up to his mouth for a kiss.

"Shall I drive you back?"

"That will not be necessary. The horse knows the way."

"Aye, old Nelly is almost older than I am. She would manage the route blind, I imagine."

He kissed the top of her head.

"I will be back for dinner."

She nodded and he ordered the mare to go. Margaux was suddenly overcome with an eerie feeling all the way back to the house. It felt like someone or something was watching her. It was a beautiful summer day, but she felt the hair on the back of her neck rise. She looked about but could see nothing. Was she imagining things? Perhaps she was simply overwrought. It had been an exhausting couple of weeks. She was on Craig land and no harm should befall her here between the barn and the house. Even as she pulled up in front of the castle and entered, she could not shake the disturbing feeling.

~

Dinner was a family affair. The children had been invited to attend, followed by some dancing in the parlour afterward. The girls were eager to show off their new talents. Margaux had loved being allowed to eat with the adults when she was a child, and she was delighted her mother was treating the Douglas girls as she had her own. Her mother was fond of children and had a natural affinity for drawing them to her.

Lady Ashbury spoke only French with them, and they were picking up an impressive amount in the short time she had been teaching them. She had made Margaux's task simple—if her voice would comply.

They were gathered in the music room, and the chairs had been moved to the perimeter of the floor. Catriona was to partner Lord Ashbury, and Maili was with Gavin. Lady Ashbury sat at the pianoforte, leaving Margaux and Aunt Ida to watch.

Her mother began to play a tune, and the girls comported themselves rather well for their first audience. Catriona showed great promise as an elegant young lady, and Maili promised to be the life of the party as she tugged and swung her partner with gusto.

Margaux tried not to chuckle as Maili was trying so hard to do just as Lady Ashbury instructed. Her mother would occasionally call out commands and shortened the dance considerably to save the men's toes.

Margaux wished she could dance. She had thoroughly enjoyed waltzing with her husband, but she knew there would be none in a country ballroom. She sighed and watched them now, attempting a jig. The laughter was infectious, and Margaux could not help but tap her toes and gently clap along. Aunt Ida decided to join in once the jig started, and pulled Margaux to her feet to partner her. Neither of them was fit enough to dance properly, but they did what they could and Margaux found herself smiling for the first time, it seemed, since the fire.

During one of the turns, Margaux suddenly found herself partnered with her father, and the next, her husband. She expected him to carry her back to her seat since she was beginning to wheeze, but instead he smiled at her warmly.

"It is a pleasure to see you smile again, wife."

She could not talk over the music, so she nodded and smiled again. He looked down at her with a look she had not seen before and it made her tingle all over. He pulled her close and danced more slowly with her. It was only family, after all, and she was very tired. The music became livelier and they turned their heads to the sounds of giggling and laughing.

Her father had Maili on his back and Catriona was swinging in his elbow. She had not seen him thus since she was a small girl. Then he had managed to dance with all three of his daughters at once. Aunt Ida was dancing happily on her own. Margaux's heart was filled with contentment at the scene. She was not sure how ready the girls were for a ball, although it would likely be more a country dance than a grand London ball—even despite her mother's involvement in it. The villagers and children were allowed to dance, and they would not have been taught by the grand masters.

When the song finished, the girls took tea with them and then it was time for them to go to bed. She watched Gavin being tender with the girls, as he hugged and kissed them goodnight before they left with their nurse. Margaux was envious, for she wished he would be that way with her. To be fair, he was kind and gentle. She was actually rather fortunate in her circumstance and she knew she should be grateful.

She snapped out of her musings when Tallach entered the room with a message.

"It is a letter from the Runners," Gavin said as he perused the note.

"Runners?" Margaux asked with surprise.

"Aye. Your father hired them to track down the Mulligans."

"What does it say?" Lord Ashbury questioned.

"Little. They have been unable to track them beyond the immediate area. Either they have escaped to Ireland, or they have not left the vicinity." Gavin handed the letter to Ashbury.

Margaux thought about her feeling of a presence earlier that afternoon, which she had dismissed. Surely they would not be so bold as to watch her in broad daylight, on Craig land, no less. They had managed to kill someone with their vengeful ways. She shuddered, thinking about the fire and her own near-death. She still could not understand why they had wanted to harm her or the orphans.

"I will tell them to keep searching. To Ireland if necessary," Lord Ashbury announced.

"Aye. They shouldna be left out there to cast their own judgements upon the people."

The next morning, Margaux was awake with the dawn, unable to sleep, for her mind was in turmoil. The weather was foul for a summer's day, but seemed to match her mood. The winds were howling and the clouds promised downpours, but she needed some fresh air. She would stay near to the house, of course; she was not fit enough for anything more. She longed to ride freely through the countryside, but she dare not try it yet.

She put on her sturdy boots and a thick cloak, should she be caught in the rain. She was drawn toward the water of the loch, and made her way along the path beside the house. If she could see it from her apartment, it could not be too far. She walked for some time, feeling her frustrations begin to ease. She was starting to tire and her chest was tightening. She found a boulder to sit on, and as she looked around, she acknowledged her vulnerability at being alone and apparently much further from the house than she had realized. When she thought of her eerie feeling the day before, she cursed her stupidity and wished she had told someone where she was going. She was too tired to make her way back and sat for some time, feeling uneasy, imagining that every animal noise or howl of the wind was the Mulligans come back to finish what they had started.

Imagining every grave possibility as the outcome of her stupidity was neither helping her breathing nor easing her exhaustion. She needed to make her way back to the house, and decided she could sit there no longer. If she put one foot in front of the other enough times she would eventually arrive.

A loud crack of thunder sent her searching for safety and her heart racing frantically. She knew a deluge was soon to follow and sought for shelter with her eyes. She could not run if she wanted to. The first drop of water hit her nose, and seeing no hiding place, she pulled her cloak over her head and slowly continued walking. The rain began to beat down upon her forcefully and she tried not to cry. She had only wanted some fresh air, but she had no one to blame but herself. She wished with her whole heart that she could go back in time and be well again. She did not look as bad as she felt inside. Her breathing became increasingly difficult until she had to rest on the muddy ground.

She heard more thunder and hoped to God that lightning would not find her as its target. Their family had lost one of its stablemen to a strike when she was a child, and therefore she had a frightening respect for Mother Nature. Not enough to have stayed inside this morning, she chastised herself, and stood up to continue.

Suddenly, a galloping horse was upon her before she could hear it over the storm or move out of the way. She was grabbed and hurled upon the horse and she tried to scream, but it was pointless, even if she'd had a voice. She tried not to panic as her heart pounded with the horse's gallop, and braced herself for death.

CHAPTER 15

*M*argaux closed her eyes and waited for the murderer to throw her off a cliff. What a perfectly Gothic, novelette-style to die. She deserved no less at this point. She had suspected someone wished to harm her, yet she had ventured out alone. She waited for the inevitable as the horse's hooves beat furiously on the muddy earth.

Suddenly, they pulled into a stable, by the smell of it. Where had she been taken? It was a relief to be out of the soaking rain. She was still too afraid to open her eyes, and she was shaking with terror.

"What is the matter, lass? I see you've had a fright, likely akin to the one I had when I discovered you were out by yourself in the storm."

Her husband's voice gently chided her as she was let down off his horse and carried into the house. He pulled off her damp cloak and wrapped his warm arms around her.

"You've not come to any physical harm, have you?" he asked, as he looked her over from head to toe.

She shook her head as her teeth chattered.

"Have a warm bath prepared in my lady's chamber," he directed the servants as he carried her up to their apartments and began to unbutton her wet gown. She opened her mouth to protest, but remembered her maid had been reassigned to the kitchen, since the girl could not bear to look at her.

When the back of her gown was undone, Gavin put his ear next to her chest to listen for her breathing. Of course, she often forgot he was a physician when she worried he would see her unclothed.

"Your lungs do not sound worse," he said, with apparent relief in his voice. He was marching to the other side of the room to fetch an elixir. "However, I am guessing you did not take your medicine this morning, by the sound of things deep in your chest."

She shook her head while still looking down. He walked back to her and sat next to her. He lifted her chin and looked in her eyes.

"Doona scare me like that again, lass. You took twenty years off my life, I swear."

He handed her the elixir, which she swallowed without protest. She was still shivering.

"You need to get warm. Do you want me to help you, or call someone else?" he asked as he removed her bandages.

"I can m-manage," she stammered through chattering teeth.

"Your face is almost completely healed. It appears that Lady Easton's salve is miraculous after all."

He reached up and gently ran his hand over the place on her cheek. It was sensitive and the intimate gesture sent a different type of shiver through her. Her husband was looking down at her as if he meant to kiss her. She saw the hesitation in his eyes before he pulled away. Her heart sank. Why did he hesitate, and what could she do about it?

"Gavin," she whispered and reached up with her hand to his, before she saw it was the ugly scarred one and quickly withdrew it, ashamed. There was a knock on the door, interrupting anything further between them.

Her husband sighed loudly. "Enter."

A maid came in.

"The bath is ready for her ladyship, m'lord. And three carriages have just arrived."

"In this storm?"

"Aye, m'lord. Lord and Lady Ashbury are downstairs, greeting them."

"Verra good. I will be there shortly after I have attended to my wife and changed."

The maid bobbed a curtsy and closed the door behind her. He stood and helped Margaux to her feet. He helped her out of her damp gown.

"I can manage the rest. Look after yourself." She smiled a little. "I am sorry I gave you a fright."

He reached up and touched her cheek again.

"You are safe, now. I will send Catriona to help you dress."

He walked through the door to receive the guests. Safe, he said. But was she? She wondered as she slipped into the heavenly reprieve of the bath.

Gavin changed his dress and hurried down the stairs to greet the newcomers. Heavens above, he hoped they were the veterans whom Easton had sent. He needed their help now more than ever. He was weeks behind on the malting process; only the day before they had cleared the drying floor for the fresh barley. He had not begun seeing to the tenants, and he wanted to devote more time to his wife and his girls, a luxury he had not been able to afford. He thought his wife might be softening toward him. Had he imagined she would have welcomed his kiss just now? He shook his head. That was not part of the bargain they had made and he would do well to remember it. She was grateful for his rescue and nothing more. He had no time to dwell on his marriage as he reached the drawing room and was greeted with merry chatter.

He entered the room, and to his surprise, there were at least half a dozen new arrivals. He recognized several of the men, having spent a fair amount of time at Wyndham and having treated many for their injuries. There was an apparent family of a husband and wife, and a daughter who appeared to be of an age that made her fit to be a governess. Lady Ashbury was in discussion with them, and Lord Ashbury was making himself acquainted with the other men.

Gavin felt a weight lift from his shoulders.

"Guid day. I am Gavin, Lord Craig, and welcome to our home. You are *very* welcome!" he announced and bowed. He smiled toward the veterans he recognized, and walked over to greet the family.

"Lord Craig, may I present Mr. and Mrs. Potts, and their daughter, Miss Alexandra Potts. They will be our new houseparents, and she will be the girls' governess and teach some at the school. She may desire to live at Breconrae with them if you have no objection? When Margaux is healed, she will likely wish to oversee many of the girls' lessons."

"Welcome. We are delighted to have you."

"I was just telling them that you might be called upon to assist in complicated medical cases when the midwife requires."

"Indeed. I would prefer that to most of my duties here. Mr. and Mrs. Potts, is this your first time working with children?"

The man's face flushed. Gavin had not meant to embarrass him.

"Yes, my lord," the man answered with a gentleman's accent.

"Mr. Potts has training in architecture. He will be helping to oversee the rebuilding, while Mrs. Potts and Miss Potts will look after the girls," Ashbury explained.

"Ah. Verra good. If you need anything, please doona hesitate to ask."

Mr. Potts seemed to relax. Gavin nodded to them and turned to greet the veterans, as Mrs. Ennis brought in a tea tray filled with sandwiches and fresh scones. Gavin directed everyone to have a seat while their accommodations were readied and their luggage sorted.

"I recognize all of your faces from Wyndham, but you must tell me your particular talents off the battlefield. I am certain I have more than enough work for everyone. Lieutenant Holdsworth?"

Lieutenant Holdsworth was missing an arm and leg, and had been left for dead at Waterloo. He was one of the soldiers Lord and Lady

Fairmont had rescued from a Belgian hospital. He appeared to be the spokesmen for the group.

"I am intended to be your new steward, if it pleases you, my lord. I was raised on a sizeable estate, and prepared the accounts for my father, the squire." He looked away as he said this, leaving the obvious unspoken. His family had not known how to handle his injuries, even though his mind was still capable of performing when his body could not.

Holdsworth was well spoken, and Gavin was sure he would be perfect for the job.

"Private Billings and Sergeant Scott are handy with their hands and can be put to use in the fields or wherever there is need. Billings is near deaf, and Scott is happy as long as he is near Billings. Served in the same regiment," Holdsworth offered by way of polite explanation.

Gavin smiled and nodded to them both, though Scott did not make eye contact. Gavin looked to the fourth soldier, a bonny Scot if ever he'd laid eyes on one. Why had he not remembered about Buchanan? He had saved the man's leg after Badajoz, when the other sawbones would have hacked it off.

"Buchanan! You look in fine fettle, I didna recognize you," Gavin explained merrily and held out his hand.

The strapping Scot pulled Gavin into a hug and near beat him on the back with his exuberance.

"Fergive me, m'lord. I ne'er thanked 'e proper fer savin' me leg."

"You can thank me proper if you ken your way to making whisky."

"Aye, I have a gift fer it, me da always said. I wouldna be a proper Scot otherwise. Beggin' yer pardon, m'lord."

"No offence taken. I appreciate whisky, even if my father and brother handled the making of it."

"We are all pleased to be here to repay your kindness to us and are happy to have work," Holdsworth remarked.

"I think we shall deal rather nicely. Mrs. Ennis, have we accommodations prepared for everyone?"

"Aye, m'lord. Cottages are ready for each of them. However, if Billings and Scott need to be housed together, we can arrange it."

"That would be appreciated, Mrs. Ennis." Lieutenant Holdsworth answered for the men.

As the group were beginning to take their leave to find their cottages, Margaux came down to greet everyone. Catriona and Maili accompanied her and made their curtsies to the newcomers.

"Mr. and Mrs. Potts and Miss Potts, gentleman; may I present to you my wife, Lady Craig, and my wards, Miss Douglas and Miss Maili Douglas."

"Welcome to Scotland, I hope you will feel welcome here," Margaux rasped out, touching her throat self-consciously.

Gavin had to hold back a laugh as the soldiers beheld his wife for the first time. They were enchanted. Holdsworth was able to harness his admiration, but the other three stared openly with appreciation. Scott blushed as she greeted him.

Gavin noticed Margaux had taken the bandage from her face for the first time. Her skin held but a faint reminder of the burn, with new pink skin, but it would be enough for comment and disgust in a London ballroom. So would the crippled soldiers, he reminded himself. It was just that his wife belonged in high society. She was the one more out of place than these soldiers. He prayed that Lady Ashbury would hold her tongue.

"Everyone was about to retreat to their prospective homes, but I do hope you will all join us here for dinner?" he suggested.

Gavin saw a look of panic on at least three of the soldiers' faces. Margaux grabbed his arm and whispered to him.

"My lovely wife informs me that you will be too kind to refuse, even though you are weary from your journey. We will have Mrs. Ennis send over some dinner, and perhaps we may all picnic by the loch tomorrow?"

"I think that sounds wonderful, my lord," Holdsworth replied.

The new arrivals had just begun taking their leave once more, when something flew through the window, shattering glass across the room.

~

Everyone had taken refuge on the floor and made not a sound. Gavin looked up when it appeared that the worst was over.

"Is anyone hurt?"

"No, my lord." He heard several replies. He stood and looked at each person to reassure himself.

"Whatever happened? There weren't any children playing out on the lawn, were there?" Lord Ashbury asked.

"No." Gavin looked around for the object responsible for shattering the thick, mullioned window. "I would gather it was done on purpose, and the person responsible is the very man we are looking for."

"Vicar Mulligan?" Lady Ashbury asked with surprise.

"At least we know they are in the immediate area," Lord Ashbury said thoughtfully.

Gavin found the good-sized rock and picked it up. It bore the words, *An eye for an eye. The whore must die.*

He controlled his anger with difficulty. He most certainly did not want his wife to see the words. What had been done to warrant an eye for an eye?

"Are we in any danger that we should know about?" Mr. Potts spoke up.

"I doona ken. There was a fire at Breconrae, and we suspect the recent vicar and his wife of starting the mischief. There has been nothing more since then."

"We have set the Runners on their trail. Now that we know they are in the area, we should have an easier time tracking them down." Lord Ashbury tried to reassure the new arrivals.

"I will set up a watch. No one is to go anywhere alone." Gavin looked at his wife pointedly. She nodded her head and he noticed her face heating.

"We will help," Holdsworth offered, and the other men nodded.

"Let us retire to the study to discuss this," Lord Ashbury suggested. Of course, Gavin reflected, the ladies were present.

The men assembled in Gavin's study and he shut the door. He

indicated for them to take a seat and he paced the room, still holding the rock.

He took a deep breath and held the rock out. Lord Ashbury was the first to step forward and take it from Gavin. He sucked in a deep breath.

"God above, this is intended for Margaux!"

"I'm afraid so."

"She has done nothing to warrant this treatment. She was staying at Breconrae with a chaperone. Even if the Mulligans disapproved of our choice to house abused girls who were impregnated through no fault of their own, why single her out instead of me?"

"I've no idea the working of the mind of zealots. I've yet to find them rational."

"Either way, we have to deal with them before they hurt her more than they already have."

"Agreed."

"I will send for the Runners and inform them to narrow their search. I think everyone should stay here so we can concentrate our efforts and guard Margaux."

"I canna believe this. I wish we had a drawbridge to shut ourselves in." Gavin shook his head.

"I do think we should go out and investigate, to see if they left any evidence and how we can best guard against any future attacks."

Lord Ashbury walked to the desk and began to write a message to the Runners.

Gavin looked toward the newly arrived soldiers. "I am sorry. You thought you were coming to Scotland to have a quiet life, and all I've given you is another battle to fight."

"Nay, m'lord. A purpose."

CHAPTER 16

*H*ow had her life come to this? She had come here to escape society and its vipers, and now she was being persecuted in rural Scotland. Gavin had not said the rock through the window was intended for her, but it surely wasn't an accident. This had become a nightmare. She had married a man who did not love her, she was disfigured, and would never be welcomed in polite circles again without whispers or disdain. Her mind went to the poor soldiers who had just arrived. How dare she indulge in self-pity!

Perhaps she should set Gavin free, she considered. She had certainly been no bargain thus far; more like a burden. He was too honourable to be anything other than kind to her, but she had seen his hesitation earlier when he wouldn't kiss her. Could she bear a marriage with a husband who could feel no more than kindness for her? Many were not so fortunate as to have that. She did not want to be the object of pity. She did not think her parents would object now if she asked to leave.

There was a soft knock on the door. She had retreated to her room after the rock had shattered the window. That, coupled with the storm and rescue, had unsettled her. She had calmed herself to greet the newcomers, but she had still been trembling inside. Then the rock had almost shattered her nerves completely.

She rose and answered the door.

"I wanted to see how you were before I go out for a while." Her husband carried in a tray of tea and biscuits. She looked at him questioningly.

"Where are you going in the mud?"

He hesitated to answer. Had her question been impertinent?

"We are going to look about and see if we find any sign of the Mulligans, or whoever is determined to harm you."

She turned away and sucked in her breath. It *had* been intended for her.

Gavin placed his arms on her shoulders.

"I willna let them harm you."

"Why are they doing this? What have I done?" she asked as she hugged herself with her arms.

"Nothing, lass. Nothing. There is a special corner of hell for hypocrites and people who misrepresent the holy word. Until they are found, I doona want you to go anywhere alone."

She thought in silence before speaking quietly. It still pained her to talk.

"I think I should go to the convent, after all."

"You are not going anywhere," he said with surprising conviction.

"If I am gone, then you won't be in danger here."

"It isn't safe."

"Do you wish for an annulment?" she asked bluntly, though it hurt her more than she thought it would to voice the question aloud and she was afraid of his answer.

"Why would you think that, lass? Have I been a poor husband?" He dropped his arms from her shoulders. "Doona answer that. I ken I have."

She spun around. "No."

She had hurt his feelings. She could see it in his face.

"Promise you willna leave. We can discuss everything else once the Mulligans are caught."

149

He turned and closed the door without looking her in the eye. What had she done? She thought it would be a relief to him. She had been nothing but a burden. Had she just ruined her chance for happiness?

~

Gavin wanted to scream. Gentle, kind, mild Gavin wanted to break something. He had been given the simple task of providing for and protecting his wife and he had failed. She had lost faith in him already and wished to annul their marriage. He had not thought the Mulligans would attempt further violence after they had murdered Mrs. Bailey, but now they had been bold enough to attack on his own land. He would never forgive himself if anything else happened to Margaux. He could not blame her for wishing to leave him, but he had fallen in love with her and he was going to prove himself to her. She might never return his love, but he would do his best to make her happy. With determination, he entered the room where the men had gathered to go and search for the Mulligans.

The room was nearly full of all of those they could gather from the nearby estate and farms. The Runner who had been searching the local area was present and took charge. Gavin was grateful. He was too angry to think clearly. It would take all of his effort not to strangle the Mulligans when they were found. Hippocrates must be turning in his grave.

"We need to make a thorough search out from the castle. Each of us will be responsible for an area from the house to the fence. Take note of anything at all—footprints, a scrap of fabric—anything that may seem inconsequential to you could mean something later. Understand?"

"Aye." The men all assented.

"Holdsworth will be in the study. Report back to him when you are finished. I've called the other Runners in, and will have them start further out and move toward us. I need to know about any abandoned cottages, caves or anywhere nearby where they could be taking shelter. Holdsworth will be interviewing the servants, in case someone saw anything, or knows of anyone who could be hiding them in the village."

"I will offer a reward for anyone who can help us," Lord Ashbury announced. "No one is safe until they are found." They had not told everyone the threats were directed at Margaux.

"I will double the reward for whoever captures them," Gavin added.

The men murmured amongst themselves and set out with determination. Gavin and Lord Ashbury took the area starting from the broken window, along with a Runner. There were heavily sunken boot prints outside the drawing room window, as if someone had stood and watched for some time. Gavin shivered at the thought. The attacker had been watching them. Thank God they hadn't found Margaux on her own this morning before he had.

"You can see where he stood, and then where he stepped back to hurl the rock," the Runner pointed out.

"How did he manage the force to propel the rock through the window?" Gavin wondered aloud.

"There are the footprints from where he ran away, but they are lost in the grass. They head toward the trees," Lord Ashbury remarked.

"I suggest we follow in that direction. Perhaps we may pick up a trail again if the rain hasn't washed it away," the Runner suggested.

"Do you think they willna realize they left prints?" Gavin asked as they headed toward the trees, searching the area around them as they walked.

"Who knows what people do in these situations," the Runner explained. "These were not hardened criminals, according to the village gossip. I think he or she snapped when Lord Craig dismissed them. Begging your pardon, m'lord."

"Nay. I know I acted out of haste," Gavin said meekly. "I will carry the blame for Mrs. Bailey's death and my wife's burns to the grave."

"You did the right thing, Craig. Do not question or blame yourself. I know Margaux does not. You cannot know what evil people hide behind. Especially a man of the cloth," Lord Ashbury said with conviction.

Gavin was not as certain his wife did not blame him.

"We have to find them," Gavin whispered. He was beginning to feel desperate. It was more real now that they had attacked his house, too. Before, he'd had no proof it had been a deliberate act.

"We are headed toward Breconrae," Lord Ashbury noticed as they reached the rock fence between the properties.

"Have you seen any more prints?" Gavin asked.

The Runner shook his head. "I was hoping to pick up the trail again. We will need to expand the search, but let us see if any of the others have found anything. M'lord, have you any hounds? They might be able to pick up a scent."

"Aye. Iain kept a pack. I am sure they would be of help."

The hounds had been unable to pick up the scent. They had tried for the rest of the day. Either the rain had washed it away, or the rock did not hold enough odour for them to track in the first place. Gavin directed the Runner to the vicarage to see if anything could be found to assist their quest.

The other men had found nothing in their search, and Gavin was having difficulty remaining optimistic. The perpetrator had waited long enough between the fire and throwing the rock that he had let down his guard. Would they do the same again? He could not credit the Mulligans with so much sophistication. It was more likely they were becoming short of funds and desperate. The thought gave him chills. He passed a restless night, wondering what else he could do.

With several men keeping watch, and the Runners searching, Gavin had to proceed with the harvest. The rest of the world did not slow down for his troubles. He did not want to stop living due to fear, but it was not only himself he was concerned with. He had a wife and children he was responsible for. He could not bear the thought of losing Margaux. He prayed the Runners would be more successful, and the men would be able to protect her.

The ball was only a few days away, and it would be nigh impossible to ensure the safety of his wife with so many people about. He could not lock her in her room, could he? Tempting as it was, that would not go down well with her.

Wallace was teaching Holdsworth, and Buchanan had been studying the whisky recipes and taking charge of the distilling at the barn. Gavin had yet to make the rounds to meet the tenants and hand deliver the ball invitations as was the custom. He could no longer delay. Normally, the lady of the manor would accompany him on such an errand. Would Margaux be safe with only him to guard her? If he took the closed carriage and stayed on the main path, perhaps. Would she be willing? Would the villagers be offended if he left her behind? Their lack of welcome of her at church made him wonder. But she was Lady Craig now, and she had been grievously injured. He had to remind himself often, for she did her best to hide that fact.

He entered the breakfast room to find her, but she wasn't there. She had not been in her room, either.

"Tallach, would you know where Lady Craig is?"

"Aye, m'lord. She is with the ladies in the parlour, assembling the tenants' baskets for the ball."

"Verra good, Tallach. Would you please call the carriage?"

He stood at the door and watched his stunning wife as she worked and oversaw the packing of the goods for the villagers. She and her mother spoke French with Catriona and Maili, who watched her with adoration. He understood the feeling. She was graceful and elegant, even with her bandages. He admired her determination despite her troubles. She certainly had ample reason to hide away and sulk, yet she was working to help him—the husband who kept letting her down. Would he ever feel worthy? Ever be worthy? God, he hoped it would be so. He had let his guard down and fallen in love again. No, he was not sure he had ever been in love before. It had not felt like this.

His wife caught him staring at her and blushed. He would not apologize. She would have to become accustomed to him adoring her. She needed to know how he felt. Perhaps that would make her want to leave even more, or perhaps she thought him indifferent. He was not.

He walked toward her.

"I am going to the village to deliver the invitations. Would you care to join me?"

He saw the look of panic cross her face. He took her arm and led her away from the others.

"You doona have to if you are not comfortable. It is a tradition, but they will understand if you are not well enough."

"No. I will go. Let me fetch my bonnet."

She was magnificent. She would have made an excellent soldier. She mastered her fears and faced them as well as anyone he had ever seen. When she had returned, he took her arm and went out of the front door.

"The carriage has a broken wheel, m'lord," a footman announced as Gavin and Margaux stepped out and saw the gig instead of the closed carriage.

"That is strange. It hasna been used since I returned from Alberfoyle."

"No, m'lord," the groom answered.

Gavin felt a moment's unease, but did not know what to make of it. Was it a coincidence the carriage's wheel was broken? Thank heavens it had been noticed before they were riding in it down the slope to the village. Recollection of Iain and his family's demise in a carriage accident gave him an ill feeling. It must be coincidence, he reasoned. He did not want to take Margaux in the open conveyance, but he had little choice, other than to leave her home. He felt under his cloak to make sure his pistol was secured. He had never been one to carry a weapon, but times were desperate.

"Thank you for your vigilance," he said to the footman, who tried not to blush but nodded.

He helped his wife into the small gig and urged the mare on. It was a beautiful summer's day. One would never know how dreadful the weather the day before had been, if not for the soft roads.

They passed by the now-golden fields in silence. The wagons were waiting to receive the grain that would be scythed and tied into bundles. He watched Margaux look out over the harvest and back towards the house. She repeated this gesture several times. Was she looking for the Mulligans? He had also been keeping an eye open, but he couldn't see everything and mind the gig. He appreciated her awareness after wandering on her own the day before.

"Do you see something?"

"No, but I have that eerie feeling again."

"Again?"

She looked guilty.

"Yesterday and the day before, when I was out alone, I felt like someone was watching me. They probably were." She had leaned in close so he could hear her.

He felt like he had taken a blow to the gut. It kept getting worse and worse. They pulled into the village safely, and he heard her sigh with relief.

CHAPTER 17

*W*here shall we start?"

"I have no notion who anyone is," she said quietly.

"Verra well. I am not certain I ken either, but a few people remain from my days here as a youth, I collect."

He helped her down from the gig and took her arm while holding the invitations in the other. The reception they received was, in a word, strange. The villagers seemed genuinely delighted to see her husband, but Margaux only received the chilliest of greetings. No one would overtly cut Lady Craig, but they were just shy of it. Cottage after cottage, it was the same; no offers of tea, or to come inside for a cosy visit. It was acutely uncomfortable—as was the smile she kept plastered to her face.

"Is your village always so..." She couldn't think of the proper word.

"Rude?" He filled in his own word.

"I understand they are leery of me."

"But you are their patroness, for goodness' sake! I canna believe it of my people," he said with disgust, and ran his hands through his hair, dishevelling it in a most alluring fashion. She was not the only one who found her husband attractive, for the village women looked equally as enamoured of him as they displayed their contempt of her.

"I am a stranger to them. I was perhaps too forward in my independence when I arrived, determined to prove myself." She smiled. "I think they meant to send me to Jericho, not marry their most eligible bachelor."

He laughed at that.

"I had not thought of it in that light. It serves them right. Perhaps they are jealous of your beauty. These parts have never seen the like, and they doona even ken you yet."

She stared at him. He had never said such to her.

"Did I say that aloud?"

She nodded in disbelief. She had always thought beauty a double-edged sword, but when the compliment came from him, it felt genuine, as if he could see into her instead of her surface. His beauty affected people, but she had no doubt he was adored as much for himself.

"Perhaps it would have been best if I had stayed at home."

"Nay. They would have criticized you more for it. At least you show your courage, and they canna find fault with that."

They continued on, though the reception was the same. She recognized some of the ladies from the shop and some from church. She smiled and did her best to appear unaffected. Once they knew her better, they would perhaps relent if she remained. If not, they risked being cut off from their lord. If they were so foolish, she would be better off without them. It still hurt to be treated as if she were a fallen woman. She was thankful she was made of sterner stuff or it would have cut her to the core. Town society would have welcomed her once she was married, she reflected. Marriage erased virtually any wrong in their eyes. Not so, here, apparently.

She was growing weary—mentally and physically—but she was determined to see this duty through. She clung more tightly to Gavin for support and hoped he did not notice what a burden she was.

When they reached the last house, they received the only kind welcome they were to have. Gavin knocked and was let into the house by a servant. When they were shown into the parlour, they were greeted by a loud exclamation.

"Why, Master Gavin, ye are a sight fer sore eyes, lad," she said with a chuckle.

"*Muime*! I didna ken you were here," he said and affectionately wrapped the woman in a hug.

"Iain set me up in me own cottage after his bairns didna need me. Do ye be needin' *Muime*?"

"Maybe," Gavin said with a blush and realized he had not introduced Margaux. "May I introduce my wife, Margaux, Lady Craig. This is my nurse, whom we refer to as *Muime*."

Margaux nodded politely to the plump woman, who must have seen at least fifty or more summers. She seemed very warm-hearted. Even Margaux felt like giving her a hug.

"Please sit down an tell me yer news. I had heard ye were here, but I didna ken if I would see ye."

"I would have been here as fast as my horse would carry me had I ken where you were."

The woman winked and smiled. "Flummery will be rewarded with yer favourites." She rang for the maid and asked for tea and tablets.

Margaux wondered what kind of treat a tablet could be, but kept the query to herself and enjoyed watching her husband with his old nurse. She had not seen him so light-hearted. She wished she could bring him such joy. When she was paying attention again, Gavin was regaling *Muime* with how they had met at Alberfoyle, but were courting other people, who had in the end, married each other. *Muime* laughed heartily at this and wanted to know how they had come together. Margaux had to blush.

"She saved me from myself. Fate had brought us both here and I needed her. You ken about Iain," he said sadly. "We had been friendly at Alberfoyle, and she had tired of society and came here to live quietly and help with their orphans. I begged ungraciously for her to be my helpmeet and she finally accepted."

"He is too modest, *Muime*," Margaux said, in her now quiet voice. "I was being shunned in the village and needed him as much."

The old lady watched the two of them with a knowing eye, but only nodded.

"I had heard some of what ye say."

"Have you heard anythin' in the village as to why my wife is still being treated ill? Yours is the last house, and none but yours so much as welcomed us in."

The nurse paused for a moment and appeared to be thinking about what to say.

"Please do not spare my feelings," Margaux said.

"Verra well. It is the Mulligans. That woman had spread venom about ye afore she'd seen yer face. She ne'er did approve of ye taking fallen girls to Breconrae."

"I see. And now that I have dismissed the Mulligans? Do they blame her?"

"I doona ken. I have ne'er been so pleased to see the backside of their nasty arses," *Muime* said with a chuckle. "There, see? Ye best find a young, happy vicar so I can get me soul back into church. I've shocked yer wife."

Margaux could not believe what she was hearing. Why centre all the hate on her when her father had set up the home for girls?

"Ye were an easy target, lass," the older woman said, as if reading her mind. "Ye came as a wealthy lady from London, a rare beauty, to be sure, and planning to set up as independent. Ye represented evr'thin' she abhorred."

"It matters not that she is now Lady Craig?"

"It matters, but even if they dislike the Mulligans, the seed was planted and it will take time to undo her lies."

"Guilty until proven innocent." Margaux's voice sounded empty.

"Aye. I'm afeard so."

"We believe the Mulligans set fire to Breconrae and are responsible for Mrs. Bailey's death and Margaux's injuries," Gavin explained.

The older woman sat quietly, watching him intently.

"There was a fire at the dower house as well as the manor house. Only yesterday, a rock was thrown through the drawing room

159

window shattering glass amongst a crowd of my guests at our home. Thankfully, no one was hurt."

"How do ye ken it was them?" *Muime* asked.

Gavin hesitated. "The fire happened the night I had dismissed them, and also the house-mother at the orphanage had been seen in dispute with Mrs. Mulligan. Yesterday, they left a note on the rock."

Margaux turned to stare at him. He had not mentioned any note.

"Well, tell us, boy," *Muime* insisted.

"It said: *an eye for an eye, the whore must die*," he said aloud with a painful cringe.

"Mrs. Bailey was Mrs. Mulligan's sister," *Muime* explained.

"Heavens," Margaux whispered as she made the connection. "She blames me, though I did not set the fire."

She could not speak. She could not breathe. The next thing she knew she was in her husband's arms and being placed into the gig.

"I am sorry, lass. I shouldna told you. Forgive me," he pleaded.

All Margaux could think was she needed to leave this cursed place, and fast. They drove back as fast as the mare would go, but Margaux remembered little of it. She was too dumbstruck and numb to think. She tried to repress all memories of her time here, and think of her beloved home in France when she had lived in blissful ignorance and harmony with her siblings. That time before Napoleon had forced them to England and into the life she had come to despise. She closed her eyes and fought back the desire to sob. How could she fight against what she could not help and was innocent of? If people chose to assume the worst, how could she prevent it?

Soon, her husband would grow weary of defending her. She was alienating him from his village. He had dismissed their vicar because of her and her family's controversial orphanage, and he had enough on his plate without having to doctor her. She would speak to her parents. They would understand when she told them what *Muime* had said. She wanted to leave for France. It would be her gift of love to Gavin.

Margaux had said not a word on the return trip to the castle. Gavin could sense her retreating into herself and he could not blame her. This madness had to cease. He desperately wanted life to return to normal, and for her to choose to stay with him. She was rubbing her hand subconsciously, the only sign that she was inwardly in pain.

He did not know what he could say to make her feel better. He wanted nothing more than to wrap her in his arms and whisper sweet assurances in her ear, but he doubted she would welcome such obviously empty words. Would she welcome the physical affection? He did not know and he worried she would not.

They pulled between the gates, and Gavin waved to the men on guard. Margaux grabbed his arm suddenly.

"Hurry!" she said with panic.

"What is it?" he asked as he urged the mare to move faster.

"I cannot say. I feel strange again."

It was then that an arrow whizzed past their heads, narrowly missing them. Gavin pushed her down into his chest and sunk as low as he could, trying to protect them. The horse sensed something was amiss, and began to spook, voicing her displeasure with a shrill neigh. Gavin crooned to the mare, and she settled somewhat, until the second arrow caught her in the hindquarters and she reared in pain. She bolted before Gavin could stop her and they held on for dear life. The mare galloped straight to the stables. Gavin shouted for help as they came near, and for the men to go after the attacker. The grooms ran to assist them and took care of settling the horse, while Gavin held on to Margaux and ran with her into the house. He was yelling for everyone as soon as they made it through the door.

"Which way were they shooting from, m'lord?" one of the men was rational enough to ask, as the house was suddenly in an uproar of activity and the male servants were gathering.

Gavin had to concentrate. It had happened so quickly. Margaux reached up and touched his hand.

"South," she said quietly. The same direction the footprints had led, toward Breconrae.

"Aye. To the south," he directed and started to go with the men as they went to search out the killers, but his wife reached out for him.

"Stay," she commanded, yet at the same time pleading with her eyes.

Right now, he wanted vengeance. Blood. The lunatics needed to be stopped. They had dared to harm his wife and kill Lord Ashbury's housekeeper, not to mention the attempts that were still happening. He forced himself to be calm and sat down next to Margaux. He waited for her to speak once the room had emptied.

"This will stop if I leave." She took a deep breath.

"No." He spoke before he even considered.

"Think. The Mulligans are growing desperate enough to attack in daylight. What if it had been one of the children? My parents can take me away. When they realize I am gone, they will stop."

"We shouldna taken you out today in an open carriage. We will catch them soon. They grow bold in crossing into Craig property. They could see you leave and follow you. We canna take the risk. And there is no guarantee they will not redirect their anger towards others. They must be caught."

Gavin stood and rang for tea, and began to pace the room. He wanted to be out there doing something, but it was clear his wife wanted him here. He watched out of the window to the south, looking for any sign of the men out searching. The Runners had been out with the hounds again, but they had not reported back on the day's efforts.

At that moment, Lord and Lady Ashbury entered the room.

"What is the commotion, *chérie?*" Lady Ashbury crossed the room to join Margaux on a sofa.

Margaux explained to her parents what had occurred, but when she suggested leaving, both of them disagreed with her. Gavin had said not a word, but watched his wife, trying to determine her true feelings. He did not blame her for wishing to leave. Someone was trying to kill her, for heaven's sake, and he had failed to protect her. He could not quite come to terms with the fact. But, would she want to stay with him after this was all over, once the lunatics had been caught? And they would be caught, he swore to himself.

Her parents continued to try to comfort Margaux. Gavin watched on with longing, wishing he could be the one whom she wanted to console her and make her feel secure. But their marriage had been one disaster after another. Perhaps she was right. Should he force her to stay in this marriage when she clearly wanted to leave? When phrased that way…

Tallach entered the room.

"Mr. Peters is here, my lord," the butler said impassively.

"Show him in," Gavin directed.

The stout man, wearing a scarlet waistcoat to match his ruddy nose, entered the room, trying to catch his breath.

"What have you found, Peters?" Lord Ashbury asked impatiently.

"We found evidence they been stayin' in the ruins of the Dower House."

"At Breconrae?" Lord Ashbury asked incredulously.

"Aye, m'lord," Peters affirmed.

"How do you ken it was them?" Gavin questioned.

"It was obvious they left in a great hurry. But they left this behind."

The man held up a Bible and opened the page to reveal the name *Mulligan*.

"That only confirms what we already believed. They must be caught."

CHAPTER 18

*M*argaux felt a warm arm draped over her and began to panic. She tried not to move, but her heart was thumping and she could feel her chest rising with rapid breaths. She wanted to scream and run. Had she been kidnapped during her sleep? Had they drugged her or hit her unconscious? She did not feel any odd sensations or pain. She willed herself to remain calm and assess the situation. The offending arm was still, and it appeared to be coming over her from behind. She dared to open her eyes, and she appeared to be in her chamber, by the dim light sneaking its way through the curtain. Thankfully, she had not been taken away.

She bravely looked at the arm. It was definitely male. The fine hands bore a remarkable resemblance to her husband's, down to the dark hairs that covered the back of his fingers. But whatever was he doing in her bed? Had he? Had *they*? She felt no different. No, she certainly would have remembered her wedding night, would she not? She needed to move and be out of the bed before he awoke. She did not know how she felt about him being there. It would certainly complicate everything. She wondered what to do. Could she successfully manoeuvre out from under him without waking him?

"*Moi stor*," she heard him say quietly.

She froze.

"You had a nightmare," he offered, by way of explanation.

"A nightmare?" She turned over to look at him then, conscious of the fact she was only in her nightgown. Oh, how she wished she would have been away before he had awoken. It hurt, physically hurt, to see him looking at her with tender eyes and hair tousled from sleep. They were facing each other in the bed. She was rigid with embarrassment, and he was speaking as if he were talking to any old acquaintance.

"It is understandable, considering," he said quietly.

"I am sorry I disturbed you. You must not feel you need to come to me."

She looked down and he was rubbing his thumb against the back of her hand. When had he taken her hand?

"Doona be sorry. I was worried something had happened."

"Have you any news?" she asked awkwardly, trying not to be aware of lying in bed with her husband for the first time; trying to concentrate on rational thought as if this large, warm, male were not there, touching her with his bare arms.

He looked away at the question. "No, lass. I wish I had more news for you, but we will find them soon. Unfortunately, we must carry on with the harvest. I want you to stay inside and with someone at all times while I am away today."

She nodded. She did not need to be told. She would have to be dragged outside until those people were caught. She wished he did not have to leave her, but she knew the harvest was here. It also meant the ball was a mere four days hence. How were they to keep the castle safe with so many people inside?

She wrinkled her nose. Perhaps no one would come if her reception in the village was anything to judge by.

"What is it?" Gavin asked.

"I was wondering what will happen if we do not find them before the ball? Then I remembered that there are not likely to be too many people attending."

He chuckled. "I imagine the room will be bursting at the seams.

They willna turn away the chance to come to a ball, nor the castle."

He was smoothing the hair back from her face. Her husband liked to touch, she noticed. He was affectionate with the girls as well, she told herself, as her heart began to speed again.

"We will find a way to keep you safe. I promise."

Then he leaned forward and kissed her softly. She closed her eyes, expecting there to be more, but he was suddenly gone from the bed. She felt foolishly bereft and full of longing. She opened her eyes to see him bend forward before standing up to pull on a dressing gown. It was long enough to see a tantalizing glimpse of his finely chiselled back. She should not be seeing him like this. It would only make leaving harder. She wished she were bold enough to call him back to her, but she did not know if he wished for her or not. She had never before been insecure as to whether a man desired her or not. But she was no longer perfect—not that she ever was, but she did not know if she could bear being rejected by him. He would probably consent. He was male, after all, but would he regret it? No, this could not happen again.

She firmly resolved not to have any more nightmares.

The next two days, Gavin scarcely saw his wife. He did not believe she'd had any more nightmares. He left the door between their chambers open so he could hear her, but he dared not sleep in her bed again. He was only human. He had seen the look of terror on her face when she had found him there a few mornings ago, and he could not bear to be the cause of any more pain for her. But, oh, he wanted to be there. He wanted her as a real wife. What had he been thinking, to offer her a marriage of convenience? He would have to distract himself. He was gone before she rose for the day, and he near fell into bed in the evenings.

He found there was little need for him to actually help with the harvest. But he needed to be there to learn, and he wanted to support his men, both on the home farm and the tenant farms. And he desperately needed to distract himself from thinking of his wife. So he joined the ranks of the men in the field and threw himself into mind-numbing manual labour.

He could not stop churning all of the pieces of this puzzle over and over in his mind, however. There had to be more to the story than met the eye. He could not dismiss the feeling that Iain's death had not been accidental, but he had no proof or idea of how the Mulligans could have orchestrated that act and he resolved to do his best not to let Iain down, lest his death be in vain.

Holdsworth and the other veterans were also there, helping where they could, and Gavin was pleased to see that the local men were making an effort to include them. Of Buchanan's acceptance he'd had no doubt, but he was less sure of the Englishmen's and especially Holdsworth's, with his missing limbs. He need not have worried. Holdsworth was willing to work hard and treated everyone respect-fully. It was all anyone needed for respect to be returned, Gavin reflected.

For three long days, the fields were scythed and wagons loaded with sheaves. Once they were taken to the barns for drying, the wagons returned for more. The women of the village worked along-side the men, bundling as the men cut. It took a village to complete the harvest, he soon realized.

Gavin wished Margaux could have been out here to share this with him. Perhaps that was a ridiculous notion, for she was raised to be a grand lady. Yet she had not seemed to be so when they had visited in the village. He also found himself gainfully employed as a physician several times, as the careless swing of a scythe cut someone or the repetitive motions of the tools against hands caused painful blisters. He was occupied thus when the carriage loaded with their luncheon pulled up.

His heart nearly stopped when he realized Margaux had come to serve the workers. He had to stop himself from running to her side when he saw her. Instead, he walked calmly toward her, watching as she served the line of men and women who held out their plates. She was smiling and talking with them, calling them by name. They seemed to be thawing toward her, if reluctantly. She was magnificent. But she was also going to find herself killed.

He reached her side and she ignored him.

"Good afternoon, Lady Craig," he said through a false smile.

"Lord Craig." She acknowledged him, at least.

"Would you care to tell me why you have broken a promise to stay in the safety of the castle?" He bent down to whisper in her ear.

"I did not promise."

"You agreed, nonetheless. How am I supposed to make sure you are safe, out here? Have you forgotten that someone has tried to harm you at least three times?"

"I have not forgotten, but I cannot allow it to stop me from doing what I ought. I have stayed at home the past three days, feeling wretched," she said, through gritted teeth and still not looking him in the eye. "And, I did not come alone."

She continued to smile and chat with the workers. Gavin had almost forgotten the Mulligans and the threat to his wife in the midst of the harvest. The ball was to be on the morrow, and he had done nothing to prepare for her safety there. He debated scooping her up and throwing her back into the carriage. He stood, trying to remain calm and not be angry. But how was he to keep her unharmed if she was to be reckless?

He would escort her back when luncheon was over, and find Ashbury in order to forge a plan for the ball. He would say no more about her leaving the house today, for it was done. But she would have to promise to be more compliant tomorrow, or he would have no choice but to lock her away for the evening.

When the workers had finished eating and the remnants of luncheon were packed back into the carriage, Gavin climbed in after Margaux. She looked at him with surprise, but said nothing. He was still unable to speak without saying something that sounded like a childish reprimand, so he held his tongue.

When they arrived at the castle, his wife marched upstairs regally. A lady would not dare stomp, but he nearly laughed at the absurdity.

He felt as if they'd had their first argument, but with nary a cross word.

Gavin went in search of Lord Ashbury, but he was with the Potts, surveying Breconrae. He was tempted to return to the fields, but they were only clearing up, now. The servants were bustling about the house with last minute preparations for the ball. He did not know whether to run and hide or join in the chaos his life had become.

He hid in his study.

He pondered ways he could trap the Mulligans. Would it be too much of a risk? He suspected they would be sorely tempted to act at the ball, and he wanted to be prepared for such a possibility.

He thought back to the interactions he'd had with them that fateful day. They had accused him of several sins. Associating with loose women and tempting the weak with drink were the basis of the allegations, if he remembered correctly. He knew their solution to dealing with loose women. He shuddered with repulsion. Would they also decide to punish him and therefore the whole village? He should set someone to guard the barns before the Mulligans decided to take a torch to those as well.

Perhaps no lure need be set to trap them. Knowing Margaux was there, enjoying the frivolity of a ball, was likely enough to send the staunch zealots into a frenzy. The ball would be bait enough. But how would he keep Margaux safe?

He stood and felt every muscle in his aching body. He strode over to the cupboard and poured himself a dram of Craig's finest. He lifted a toast to Iain and his family as they looked down upon him from their resting place on the canvas above the mantel. What, he wondered, would his older brother tell him to do?

He and Iain had been close, yet as different as night and day. Gavin had known he was the spare and had always been able to do as he pleased. His father had purchased a commission for him as was befitting a second son, but with his medical training, he had worked as a surgeon rather than enter the cavalry as was due his name. It went against his nature to kill, so he had saved as many lives as possible in the medical tent. His father had never quite approved of his love of medicine. It was perhaps too shabby-genteel and was considered a profession. Never mind that farming was work.

Iain would likely tell him to bed his wife and that would solve all of his problems. Gavin chuckled. Iain's outlook on life had been ever pragmatic. Gavin had envied him that. Iain had preferred avoiding conflict and preserving people's feelings. Gavin longed for the simplicity of his old life. How had it come to this?

He shook his head and took a sip of his drink. The harvest had gone well, at least. If they could survive the ball, then he would turn his full attention to his wife. The veterans were beyond his expectations, and soon he would be able to leave the main running of the estate in their capable hands.

He set down his glass. The whisky was not giving him clarity on the best method for apprehending the Mulligans, he reflected. It was making him feel as if he should try to make amends with his wife. It was as good of an excuse as any to talk to her.

CHAPTER 19

*M*argaux wanted to lie on her bed and sulk, but the seamstress had come for the final fitting of her ball gown. She had no desire to see the woman again, but her mother had assured her the gown covered all of her burns and there would be no unpleasantness. Margaux was beginning to become numb to people's reactions. That was a good thing, she thought.

She needed to find the girls and spend time with them as well. Her mother had taken them under her wing, which had given Margaux time to heal, but her parents would be leaving shortly and Catriona and Maili would become her responsibility once more.

She reluctantly went to the parlour and reminded herself she was going to be indifferent. Her mother smiled and glided over to her when she entered the room.

"*Chérie*, you will adore the dress. Madame has quite outdone herself."

Margaux thought spitefully it was probably to make up for her rude behaviour before. But when she saw the gown, she almost forgave the *modiste*. It was exquisite. Being honest with herself, Margaux had not thought she would have new ball gowns again. It was part of what she had forfeited when she had decided to abandon society.

"Lady Craig." Madame curtsied deeply before her. "May I assist you into the gown?" The woman looked directly at her, and her eyes pleaded for another chance. Margaux wanted to dress privately, as she had been trying to do lately. She would call for Catriona when she could not manage on her own. She could tell the *modiste* felt remorse for her previous behaviour. She could not blame her reaction, she supposed. Would she have reacted thus if she had seen something ghastly? Maybe, but she would like to think not. She nodded her head and stepped behind the screen. She had taken care to make sure her bandages were always in place since that day when they had last met.

The gown was high-necked, which was not the normal fashion, but it was tastefully done so that it was not as large and frilly as it could have been. Instead, the neck was a flesh-coloured satin, made to appear as a false skin with a thin lace pattern on top. The underdress was a lavender colour, with an overslip to match the false neck. The colour was an acknowledgement of mourning, yet it still represented summer. It was unique and original. She had never seen anything like it.

"It is beautiful," she said with open appreciation.

"*Merci*, my lady." The *modiste* blushed.

"It must have taken hours. I do not think I have ever had anything so fine."

"It was important to me to have it perfect."

Their eyes met, and Margaux understood this to be the woman's way of apologizing. She smiled and stepped from behind the screen.

"*C'est magnifique!*" Lady Ashbury exclaimed.

"Princess!" Maili shouted and ran over to touch the gown.

Catriona and Maili were also trying on their new gowns for the evening. They were of a similar colour but appropriate to their age.

"Catriona, you look like a young lady," Margaux said appreciatively. "And Maili, you look like a princess, yourself."

"*Grand-mère* says we must behave properly to make Papa Craig proud."

Margaux looked up at her mother in surprise at hearing her called grandmother. Her mother winked back at her.

"Oh, you will make him proud. I am very proud of you, too."

She bent over and kissed each of them on the cheek.

"Now you must stand still for *Madame* to make sure everything is perfect. Then we must take off our beautiful gowns so nothing happens to them before the ball."

Maili pouted at this command, but she did as she was told.

The girls went on their way to have tea in the nursery, and her mother stayed behind with Margaux in the parlour after the seamstress departed. She could tell her mother wished to speak about something. She had that look. She sat and waited.

"*Chérie...*" Her mother paused.

"*Oui, Maman?*"

"I wanted to speak with you alone. Your father and I wish what is best for you, of course. We were delighted you found Lord Craig and married, but you do not seem happy."

Margaux looked sharply at her mother.

"It has been a difficult few weeks, *Maman*."

"*Oui*. I believe it will improve. He is a wonderful man, and he will love you with all of his heart if you give him the chance."

Margaux looked into her mother's eyes and wanted to weep. How could she tell her mother that she had made an agreement with him? That he said he could not fall in love again? Besides, she was not the same, beautiful woman he had married. Unfortunately, she had already fallen deeply, hopelessly, in love with her husband. She could not stop the tears from falling, and her mother came to her and wrapped her arms about her.

"If you wish to have the marriage annulled, we will help you," her mother said softly. She had misunderstood her daughter's tears.

"I do not know what to do, *Maman*."

"You love him," Lady Ashbury stated. Ah, she had not misunderstood.

Margaux could not look her mother in the eye, but nodded and wept the tears she had needed to weep since the fire.

"You underestimate your husband, *chérie*. You think he cannot love you because of your burns?"

Margaux nodded. "I did not look like this when we agreed to marry. How could he ever want to touch me? You see how people react to me. My maid could not even look at me!"

"Have you seen how your husband looks at you, my love? He is not disgusted by these things. He chose to be a doctor because these things do not bother him. However, your burns are healing. Your face may have a little different colour, but it is still beautiful, nevertheless."

"Not being repulsed by my burns and being intimate is quite different."

"*Oui*, it is. But you do not give your husband credit to see your real beauty. You have always been the one to feel your physical beauty was a burden. Your husband is just as handsome as you are beautiful. He must know how you feel. I believe he can see beneath your skin."

Could her mother be right? But how was Margaux to know? He had never given her any indication of more tender feelings. He had done no more than give her a chaste kiss.

"How, *Maman?*" she whispered.

"You must show him his attentions are welcome."

Margaux looked at her blankly.

"You must flirt, *chérie*. Sometimes I despair that you have no French blood in you!" Her mother shook her head.

"You want me to bat my eyelashes, and simper and fawn over him?" she asked, in disbelief.

Her mother sighed audibly and dropped her head in her hands.

"I have failed."

"I am certain you tried to teach me these things. But it was never necessary to pretend such affectations before, to know a man was interested."

"No, I suppose not. Perhaps it is Lord Craig's lack of experience in society that makes him less flirtatious. He may be intimidated by your sophistication."

"My sophistication?" Margaux asked in disbelief.

"*Oui*. You come from different backgrounds. He may be the son of a baron, but he went off to join the army, and has lived in a small village practising medicine ever since. He did not move to London and take up the life of a *ton beau*."

"True. Thank God." Margaux had not considered how she might appear to him.

"I also think you are insecure because of your burns. I think a few more smiles and simple touches will go a long way, my dear."

"I will try, *Maman*."

Her mother hugged her again and kissed the top of her head. "Besides, he will swoon when he sees you in that gown."

She laughed and rang for tea. She hoped it would be that simple.

It was dinner before Gavin saw his wife again. She was looking as beautiful as ever, sitting at the opposite end of the table. He was ready for the ball to be over, and for the nightmarish Mulligans to be caught so they could be alone and he could woo her properly. His blood ran warm thinking about it. He should most certainly not be thinking about it at the dinner table, but when he met his wife's gaze, there was something different in her look. It gave him hope.

After dinner, he met up in the study with Lord Ashbury and the other men, trying to forge a plan to keep Margaux safe.

"As uncouth as it may be, I think you need to be assigned to Margaux for the night. Meaning, appear to be besotted with your new wife and sit in her pocket."

Gavin did not find the thought distasteful at all.

"He will need to find someone to back him up if he has to attend to something," Mr. Peters, the Chief Runner, added.

"Of course," Gavin agreed.

"I agree with you, Craig, that the Mulligans will be drawn here like moths to a flame. They have been lying low for three days, but I do not think, with all of the *sinful* activity of a ball, they will be able to help themselves," Lord Ashbury said with obvious distaste.

"I remember them being vehement that I close the distillery. I believe they will try to strike there. Perhaps even as a diversion to allow them to find Margaux," Gavin said quietly.

"I agree, m'lord. I think ye should move the barrels into the dungeon. The barn is not secure enough. If they took a torch to it, the spirits would ignite in a second."

"I had not thought of that. We should move them now. Who is to say they willna strike tonight?"

"And tomorrow?"

"I would still like to have the barn guarded. They may not know we have moved the whisky and I doona want to lose an entire harvest. It would devastate the village."

"We will guard the barns, m'lord." Buchanan spoke up.

"I have assigned a Runner to each of the castle entrances," Mr. Peters announced. "Though I think there should be one way in and one way out."

"Will it be enough?" Gavin wondered out loud.

"We will need to arm ourselves, and Lady Craig, of course," he added.

Gavin looked up in alarm. He had thought if the Mulligans showed up they could be apprehended and carried off to the gaol.

"There will be a crowd. Anything can 'appen and it's best to be prepared. They will probably try to disguise themselves."

"Verra well. I will see to arming everyone," he conceded.

"We will see to moving the barrels, m'lord," Buchanan announced.

Gavin nodded. "Thank you," he said absent-mindedly as the enormity of the task struck him. There were to be many people in the castle tomorrow, yet he was terrified he would not be able to protect the one person who had come to mean the most to him in this world.

It was late by the time he went upstairs to discuss the plan with Margaux. She did not answer the knock on the dressing room door, so he cautiously peered into the room. She looked like an angel. She had fallen asleep in a chair near the hearth. The window was open and moonlight shone on her face. A gentle breeze played with a ruffle on her white dressing gown, and her black hair tumbled about her. Gavin swallowed hard. He sat on the footstool next to her for some time, watching her sleep, debating if he should carry her to the bed or wake her.

A lock of hair seemingly tickled her nose and she brushed at it with her bandaged hand. Gavin reached up and moved it back out of her face. Then her eyes were suddenly open and staring dreamily into his. He licked his lips and her thumb reached up and gently caressed the pathway his tongue had taken. Dare he take advantage of the moment?

She smiled and closed her eyes.

Gavin sighed. Apparently his wife only desired him in her sleep. He scooped her up and placed her gently on the bed. It took all of his will-power to walk back to his own room. But he refused to bed his wife until she asked him to.

CHAPTER 20

The day of the ball had finally arrived. Margaux wished she felt excitement, but instead she was shaking with terror. She forced herself to act as if everything was as it should be, to survey the hard work of the servants and be appreciative.

The baskets were finished for the tenants to take home with them, the ballroom floor was polished to a shine, the candles were in place, and the floral arrangements had been positioned to create the illusion of an indoor garden. An array of lilies, orchids, and roses had been artfully placed amongst beds of greenery. It was splendid. Her mother had outdone herself as usual. It almost looked like a normal ball, however, instead of the elaborate themes her mother created for her own home. Margaux was grateful Lady Ashbury had shown such restraint. It was likely still more opulent than anything the county had ever seen.

She went into one of the parlours next, which had been set up as a room for entertaining the children. There would also be games on the lawn, but the terrace doors would not be opened this year. The children would have to go through the front entry and walk around. Would it be obvious to the villagers that they were being guarded? Did they know the Mulligans wanted to kill her?

Gavin had come to her and informed her that she must arm herself, in case something should happen and the Mulligans sneaked past the several layers of protection they had in place. A dagger. She had been given a dagger to wear on her leg; a dagger she might have to defend her life with. She shivered.

The drawing room had been cleared of the sofas and the carpets rolled up to make way for the tables and chairs where people could eat the supper. Servants were bustling about with linens, silver, and glass, and Mrs. Ennis was directing the placement of the floral arrangements as centrepieces. It would have been exciting for Margaux to host her first ball if she had actually done the work and if she was not terrified the Mulligans would make it past the barriers set in place. How would they stop them? Gavin had warned her they might be in disguise.

She swallowed and continued on. Cook was completing the final touches on the five-storeyed cake fashioned to look like the castle, turrets and all. Margaux smiled. She could see her mother's handiwork in that. There were biscuits shaped as castles for the baskets, too.

Everything was perfect. She had known it would be, though. She went up to the nursery to see the girls, even though the climb was difficult. She remembered the first ball she had been allowed to attend, and knew they must be bursting with excitement. She was not wrong.

"Princess!" Maili ran toward her and hugged her. "Come look at the flowers *Grand-mère* has brought us. This is to dress my hair!"

"You will be the most beautiful girls there, no doubt," Margaux said fondly.

Catriona was sitting quietly in a chair.

"Good evening, Catriona."

"Good evening, Lady Craig."

She knelt down before her. "Catriona, I think it is time you called me Margaux."

Catriona looked up and smiled.

"Is something the matter?" Margaux asked. Catriona was not acting like a girl excited about her first ball.

"No. But I was wondering if we should be wearing our pretty new dresses. Will it make the other girls feel bad?"

"Oh, my dear. I don't know. That is so kind-hearted of you. But my parents are very generous with them. I imagine *Maman* has made certain they will have something special."

Catriona sighed with relief. "When we were at Alberfoyle, Lady Vernon would sometimes send us gifts and it made the other children jealous."

"I see. It cannot be helped, I suppose. Sometimes others will have things you want, too. All we can do is make sure we are kind and generous with people. If we see a need, then we must help."

Maili walked over from where she was playing with the flowers. She must have been listening.

"Do you think we could give some of our dresses to the children who need them, since *Grand-mère* ordered us new ones?"

"I think that is a perfect idea. You can observe tonight and see if there are any children you think might need them. Then you can tell me tomorrow." She hugged the girls.

"Catriona, would you mind re-bandaging my arm and neck? I want to make certain it stays in place for the night."

"Of course." Catriona rose from her chair and went to fetch the supplies. Margaux stole a glance at the wounds when the bandages were off. She was coming to terms with them, since they were now a part of her. The skin did appear to be healing. Some of it was now smooth, but there were some knotted rope-like areas that had turned purple and had puckered. They were tight and they were tender when Catriona applied the salve.

"Did I hurt you?" Catriona asked with concern.

"No, but it is very tight and sore. Papa Craig said I need to massage the area, but I am not very good at it."

"I will ask him how and make sure I help you remember," Catriona said intently.

"Thank you. I would appreciate that. Now, I must go and see to dressing myself. When you are finished, would you please come to my room and help me?"

"Oh, yes, Mama Margaux," Maili said as she danced about the room. Margaux felt a twinge in her heart at being called mama again. She smiled at Maili's enthusiasm. Oh, to be a carefree child once more.

She had to rest from the exertions of the day. She had hoped she might be able to dance at least once with her husband tonight, but she would need to conserve her energy. She had tried to distract herself from worry, but now she was alone with her thoughts. The problem was, it did no good to wonder what might happen. The Mulligans were not rational or predictable. No one in their right mind would do the things they had done. And that was what frightened her the most.

Her mother had sent her maid to dress her hair, and the girls joined her as she was finishing. Margaux had decided to have her hair curled and only secure part of it atop her head. The rest of the curls were artfully placed, partially down her back and a few over the scars on her cheek. They were not so very noticeable, and she could not hide from them forever. It would have drawn more attention if she'd had a large bandage there.

The girls were watching everything with awe. Margaux tried not to laugh. She remembered watching her own mother prepare for balls with equal adoration. The maid helped her into the gown and slippers. She felt almost beautiful again. She was grateful the scars were scarcely noticeable from the outside, but she would still know. She was certainly different on the inside.

There was a knock on the adjoining door, and Gavin entered and took proper notice of the girls in their new finery. He looked up at her and inhaled audibly. Margaux was gratified, and then ashamed that she was. But it mattered to her. She wanted to be perfect for him.

"Girls, there is someone here to see you. But first, we wanted to give you a little something for your first ball."

He handed them each a little black box, which they opened them to reveal heart-shaped pendants. Both squealed with delight and threw their arms around him. He kissed each of their cheeks.

"Let me put these on you, lasses, so you may go on downstairs."

When the girls had left, Margaux and Gavin stood staring at each other. It was hard not to blush. She eyed him as he did her. She had never seen him dressed for a ball. She had not thought it possible for him to be more handsome. His hair had grown a bit longer, enough for it to curl at the ends. She wanted to run her hands through it. He was wearing his family's tartan again, which happened to have a thread of lavender woven into it. He was perfection itself; especially when coupled with his bright blue eyes and dark hair. He made a mockery of the London dandies who would give an arm to look like he did with such little effort. He was walking toward her, piercing her with his eyes, and then he was standing before her.

"Wife," he said in a smooth, seductive voice. "You take my breath away."

Oh my. She should say something, but she was robbed of speech. She lifted her hand and gently caressed his cheek. He turned his head and placed a soft kiss on her palm. It felt as if she had been scorched. A bad pun, she thought, considering.

"I wish our presence was not required downstairs at this moment, Margaux."

He rarely spoke her name, but it felt intimate. Her mother had been right. He seemed to be responding to her cues.

He cleared his throat.

"I have something for you as well," he said, as he produced another black box. "It is from the family vault. I confess I had your mother help me choose the appropriate set." He smiled sheepishly.

She opened the box to reveal a stunning amethyst necklace and matching earrings. It was perfect. The large stone hung where the false neck of her gown was. She hoped the necklace would not draw attention to it, after all it was designed to hide, but it seemed as if it had been made for the dress. In all likelihood, knowing her mother, it had been done deliberately. Gavin finished clasping it behind her neck and he placed his hands on her shoulders. She turned to face him.

"Is your dagger in place?"

She sighed. He had ruined the moment; she had just worked up enough courage to kiss him.

"Yes."

"And you ken how to use it? Though I doona plan on leaving your side."

She made a mock demonstration of jabbing her fist into his neck. He laughed nervously and kissed her on the forehead. He held out his arm. "That will have to do. Shall we?"

When they stepped into the hallway, they met with an unexpected visitor.

"Jolie?" Margaux said with utter shock. "Is it really you?"

"So it is true, then?" her sister said none too happily as she looked from Margaux to Gavin, linked arm in arm. "How could you?"

"Welcome to our home, Lady Beaujolais. I trust your journey was uneventful?" Gavin bowed to her as if she had not just insulted them.

She looked at him, incredulous.

"You remember Dr. Craig, do you not?" Margaux asked calmly.

"I...I." The moment of recognition crossed her face. "But..."

"I have only recently come into the title on the death of my brother," Gavin explained.

"Forgive me, Lord Craig. One would think one's mother might have mentioned that minor detail. You have not quite married a stranger then, have you? I was prepared to take drastic measures."

"I entered into this marriage of my own volition, Jolie," Margaux said quietly.

"If you will pardon me, ladies, I think I would rather not be present for this conversation." He smiled and his dimples peeped out. "Shall I have trays sent up so you may continue this in private? I am certain everyone will understand as long as you are down in time for the receiving line."

"Thank you, my lord. I believe that an excellent idea," Jolie answered, and dragged her sister back into her room.

"Why, yes, Jolie, I will neglect my guests and join you in here. Thank you for consulting me," Margaux said sarcastically.

"Oh, Marg!" Her sister gathered her up in painful hug. It was all Margaux could do not to cry out. When Jolie let her go she had to take deep breaths to ease the pain.

"What is the matter? Oh! Is it the burns? Do they still pain you? You look so fine, I had forgotten."

"I am healing. The burns are still sensitive to the touch, but are thankfully hidden beneath the gown and gloves."

"Are they very bad?"

"They could have been much worse. The housekeeper died," Margaux said softly. It was still difficult to acknowledge that out loud. It should have been her.

"I knew, you know. I could sense something was wrong that night. It was horrible to know you were in danger, and I did not know what until the letter came. It took me forever to arrange a chaperone and to travel here. Then *Maman* tells me you are married! You of all, married." She held her hands wide to emphasize the enormity of the event.

"Yes."

"That is all you can say? You, who shunned a dozen eligible suitors in London; you, who objected to marriages of convenience; you, who declared you would only marry for love. I understand a little after realising you were acquainted, but can you truly tell me you formed a *tendre* for him before you married? You have never been a hypocrite."

Margaux was too angry to reply. She turned away and looked out the window. She did not have the energy to argue about why she had done it. It was done, and she did love him now. Even if it was one-sided love.

"Why are you here, Jolie? If you have come to rant at me over my marriage, then save your breath. It is done. Why should it bother you? You, yourself, are perfectly willing to marry for convenience. Or can you tell me you are in love with Yardley?"

"I never pretended to want a love-match. You made your feelings on my choice very clear before you left town. Am I to be denied the pleasure?"

Margaux sighed. "Very well. Carry on."

Jolie sagged her shoulders. "It is not as much fun if you are given permission to scold. I only want to see you happy."

"I know." Margaux walked over to her sister and took her hand.

"We all believed you would come to your senses within a fortnight," Jolie said resignedly.

"I know."

"I never could have imagined you would be married already."

"I didn't, either."

"Did something happen to make it necessary?"

"No!" Margaux dropped her sister's hand and pushed at her in a sisterly way. "Not in that way."

"Well, what are we supposed to think?"

"I suppose I came to my senses. It happened so fast. I became an instant pariah, Jolie."

"A pariah? You had a chaperone."

"Aunt Ida?" Margaux asked mockingly.

"That bad? She always was a bit flighty, but a dear."

"She is still a dear, but she is not always here, even when she is."

"Ah. I see. So the prudish little village took a dislike to an independent woman and shunned you. And you were too proud to come back to London with your tail between your legs, and Dr. Craig came to your rescue. I suppose you should be so fortunate he was not a pickled old man stuffed into creaking stays with rotten teeth."

Margaux watched her beautiful, confident sister walk about the room as she summed up the situation with alarming accuracy.

"I believe I would have come to London with my tail between my legs, as you say, before that." She laughed.

"He is extraordinarily handsome, Marg." Jolie's knowing eyes mocked her.

"He is," she agreed jovially as she could only with her triplet.

"Are you in love with him now?"

Her sister's eyes pierced through her. She did not have to answer. She lowered her eyes.

"When did you arrive? And who came as your chaperone?" Margaux decided it was more comfortable to change the subject, though she knew Jolie could see through her.

"I believe it has been a couple of hours, now. We were unaware there was to be a ball today. I had envisioned you still in the sick room. But I am relieved to know you are not."

"Only you could come straight from the carriage looking ready for a ball. It is to be the tenants' ball, however."

"I will try not to embarrass you with my London ways."

Margaux rolled her eyes.

"Yardley might."

"You brought Yardley with you?" Margaux could not believe it. "Are you betrothed?"

"No, we are not. And he insisted. As did his mother. The Season is over, and they were on their way to their country house anyway."

"Dear me. I hope you will explain later." Margaux laughed. "The villagers will be too terrified to step into the house if they know the Duke and Duchess are present."

"They will not know until it is too late. They do know how to behave," she chided.

"Do they? Around those they consider well beneath them?"

"That is unfair, Marg."

"Perhaps. He only disapproves of society, then."

"It is easy to become jaded when everyone toad-eats you all the time."

"Very well. I will give him another chance. He approves of you, so he cannot be all bad. If he makes you happy, I will try to be happy for you."

"I am not sure."

CHAPTER 21

*M*argaux walked down the stairs arm in arm with her sister. She had not realized how much she had missed Jolie. She had poured her heart out to her and told her about the crazed Mulligans and their desire to harm her. She had struggled to maintain her composure so she did not appear blotched and with a red nose before the whole village. But she felt relief, knowing she no longer held the burden of her fear and guilt of her marriage inside. If only their other triplet, Anjou, were here. Margaux knew Anjou was unharmed, for Margaux knew she would sense if her sister were in danger, but missed her nonetheless.

Everything suddenly seemed so real to her with Jolie and Yardley there. She saw him standing across the room, speaking to her father and her husband. She rarely disliked people before knowing them, but she held a very low opinion of the Duke. He would not make her sister happy. But if anything came of the courtship he would be her brother, and she must make an effort to be civil.

She scanned the room. Seamus had come for the celebration, and his sisters were adoring him and, no doubt, filling his ears with all of their adventures since coming to live at the castle. Jolie was pulling her towards the Duke of Yardley, and she knew she might as well have it over with.

"Welcome to our home, your Grace. I trust you had a pleasant journey?" she asked, while offering him her hand, though her voice was still strained. She was going to be hoarse again before the night was half over.

"Lady Craig, I can see you have received excellent medical attention. I am pleased we find you recovering." He took her hand and grazed a kiss over her fingers.

Margaux had to fight a blush. Yardley was behaving in a kind and gracious manner. What was he about? She wondered, although she knew she was being unkind.

"Thank you, sir. Forgive our tardiness."

"Forgiven. I understand the need to keep your sister to yourself."

He gave her sister a knowing look. Margaux was going to be ill.

"I must greet the Duchess, if you will excuse me."

"May I join you?" Gavin asked as he took her arm and led her into the ballroom where the servants were lighting the last of the candles and the musicians were tuning their instruments.

She smiled at his rhetorical question since he had already led her away. She noticed her mother speaking with the Duchess of Yardley and Aunt Ida near the terrace. It was going to be unbearably hot with the terrace doors closed and a full room of exuberant dancing.

"How are you feeling?"

"I am trying to remain calm. It is nice to have my sister here. It makes the situation with the Mulligans seem like a nightmare I needed to wake up from."

"I am glad she is here for you, but do not let down your guard tonight. I have told Yardley of the situation, but we will remain discreet. I do not want word getting out and everyone panicking. Besides, we do not know who is on their side. Someone must have been helping them."

Margaux swallowed. She had not considered that. Would someone betray her? Many of the villagers did not like her. Many might feel as the Mulligans did.

"There is a Runner at each door, though only the front entrance is open," her husband was saying.

"Do the Runners know what the Mulligans look like? They cannot have seen them before," Margaux asked as the thought suddenly occurred to her.

Gavin's face paled. "Dear God. No, of course they have not. Forgive me. I must speak with them."

She watched her husband move out of the room with haste, so she made her way to greet the Duchess on her own, pretending that she was happy to be there, and that the Mulligans were not trying to kill her.

When it was time to form the receiving line, Gavin informed her that he had taken some of the servants from their posts to help guard the front door. She felt her self-control threaten to abandon her. She was at someone else's mercy, someone who had tried to kill her more than once. She pasted her best smile to her lips and stood in the line.

As they greeted the guests, no one was as openly hostile as they had been the first day in the village. No one was friendly either. It was an improvement.

When the time came for the dancing to begin, Gavin indicated for Yardley to do the honours with her sister.

"Margaux canna dance yet, and I will remain by her side."

"I cannot ask you to sit out every dance for me, my lord," Margaux protested.

"In normal circumstances, I might be persuaded, but tonight I willna leave you. It is not such a bad bargain, my lady." He smiled down at her and her stomach did a flip.

All she could do was nod.

He led her around the floor and introduced her to some of the nearby gentry who had come from beyond the village. They watched the dancing become more boisterous and loud as the evening progressed, after the completion of the stately opening quadrille. Some of the older children joined in the dancing, and the drawing room was filled with many of the younger ones playing games. The room was suffocating to her, and she wanted the night to be over.

There were five sets of dancing before the supper began. Once the plates were filled and most everyone had taken their seats, Gavin tapped his glass with a fork to make an announcement.

"Guid evening, everyone, and thank you for joining us to celebrate another successful harvest. It is a time of mixed emotions for us, having just lost Iain and his family, but he was a jolly fellow and would have been offended if we'd cancelled the ball on his behalf. I raise my glass to him and to you."

"Hear, hear" the crowd echoed.

"And to my lovely wife, who I doona doubt is having second thoughts about marrying me after all, but I have hope, since she hasna left me yet."

He dimpled and gave her a sheepish grin. Margaux's knees felt weak.

"If you willna mind the liberty, I intend to have a waltz played so my wife may join me for one dance this evening. She is still recovering, but her doctor will allow this one exception."

He winked at her. She felt her face flush. There were a few chuckles and a few murmurs, but she hoped the villagers would understand.

Gavin held his hand out to her and she placed her hand in his. She could feel her heart racing, but whether it was from her husband's touch or the crowd watching them she did not know.

But when the music started and her husband placed his hand on her waist and took her bandaged hand gently and held it to him, she lost herself in the moment, allowing herself that small glimpse of heaven. Their eyes met and held. She never wanted the dance to end.

She was partially conscious of being joined on the floor by a few other couples swirling about in their periphery; Yardley had led Beaujolais out, her parents were there, and a few of the local gentry who knew the dance. The villagers stood and watched—some admiring and some disapproving, to judge by their expressions. Margaux could not care in that moment. It was glorious to be in her husband's arms.

And then, Margaux knew *they* were there. She could feel it. But where?

"What is it?" Gavin asked. She must have become tense.

"I feel them." She was barely able to speak the words.

Gavin looked up and began to scan the room. She also tried to look about. There were so many faces unknown to her. The Runners hadn't ever seen them, had they? How could they be expected to keep them away? She began to break out in a cold sweat.

"Keep smiling. Act normally until we find them," he said, looking down to smile at her.

"How will we find them before it is too late? There are too many people here."

"I am going through each face one by one. I gave the signal to Peters and he is combing through the crowd as we speak. Doona leave my side."

She nodded and tried to calm herself with deep breaths, though she felt as if no air were making it to her lungs. Her body was trembling despite her best efforts to control it. Gavin swirled her to the edge of the room and kept her there, surveying the throng with every turn.

Lawn bowls, bag and spoon races, oranges and lemons, draughts, and an area for dancing...what should she try next? Maili surveyed the almost chaotic scene with bliss. And to think she lived here! She still had to pinch herself to believe she wasn't dreaming. Alberfoyle had been pleasant enough, but she had longed for a family again. And now she had one.

As she waited her turn for a game of draughts, she spied the table with desserts and decided it was impossible to have too many ices, though she had already indulged in one. She watched Catriona dancing a jig with a local boy she had never seen before, and decided to peek through the terrace doors to watch the adults. She sighed wistfully as she caught a glimpse of Lord and Lady Craig waltzing. The two of them, arm in arm, fitted every picture of a fairy tale in her young mind.

Maili turned when she heard something sounding like a yelp then a whimper in the nearby hedge close to the gardener's shed, and walked over to investigate. Mayhap an animal had been caught up that needed help. As she drew near to the shed, a dirty older woman came out from behind it.

"M-m-may I help you?" Maili asked nervously, instantly stepping back from the woman who had strange eyes and messy hair. She searched in vain for her nurse, wondering what she should do.

"I need you to take me to Lord Craig! My husband is hurt and I need help!" she exclaimed.

Without another thought Maili took the woman's hand.

Peters was waiting for Gavin when they made it to the side of the ballroom.

"Have you news, Peters?" Gavin asked anxiously.

"Maili's nurse cannot find her," the Runner said as quietly as he could in the noise-filled ballroom.

Gavin sucked in his breath. It had never occurred to him that the girls could be in danger. "Do you think they have taken her?"

"I don't know, m'lord. But we have not found her in with the other children and we wanted to inform you straight away."

Gavin nodded absent-mindedly, searching his brain for ideas. He should not panic. It was not likely that Maili had been taken.

Margaux touched his arm. "Does Catriona know?"

Peters nodded. "The nurse found her first before coming to me. I've sent the guards to scour the grounds."

"We need to search the house before we panic," Gavin suggested, though he could feel Margaux's tension when she heard the guards were no longer at the doors.

"She might have gone to her room or to the nursery," Margaux suggested. "I can ask Jolie to go with me."

"No. You will not leave my side. We can ask your mother."

Margaux nodded and began searching the crowd for her parents.

Suddenly the crowd began to part and the music stopped—along with Margaux's heart. For there, hand in hand with Mrs. Mulligan, was Maili.

"Oh, God," she whispered.

"Stay calm, *mo grádh*," Gavin said quietly, keeping his eyes focused on Mrs. Mulligan.

"Maili," Gavin said, with a calm he did not feel, and held out his hand to his girl, who clearly had no idea of the danger she was in.

"Not so fast," Mrs. Mulligan hissed. The woman pulled Maili to her in a vice-like grip about both arms, and the little girl yelped with pain. The woman held a gardener's dibble in her other hand.

"Please, Mrs. Mulligan. Your complaint is with me, not an innocent child." Gavin attempted to reason with the woman, who had clearly lost all sense of reality, as she did not appear to have bathed or combed her hair in days. Maili began to cry, the noise resounding in the otherwise silent ballroom. The entire crowd stood paralyzed, watching with horror as their beloved Mrs. Mulligan stood demon-like before them. Most were unaware what their vicar and his wife had done to Margaux and the orphans.

The woman looked to Margaux and spat at her.

"Jezebel!"

The woman was possessed. Gavin had occasionally seen soldiers lose their minds on the battlefield, and he knew there was no point in trying to reason with her. He did need to pry Maili from her arms before she could be apprehended. The only place for her was an asylum.

"This woman has been sent by the devil! He sent this temptress to ruin you and corrupt you!" Mrs. Mulligan was ranting, her eyes glazed and unseeing.

"Mrs. Mulligan," Gavin said gently, "may we go outside and talk about this?"

"No! You have been seduced by her lies. I don't want to talk! She must be punished!"

"What do you mean, Mrs. Mulligan?" Gavin asked, in what he hoped was a soothing voice.

"The devil must die!"

The devil, meaning Margaux.

Gavin had to remain calm. He could feel Margaux trembling beside him, but she had not said a word. This needed to end quickly, but the village needed to see him try to do what he could for her.

"Mrs. Mulligan, where is the vicar?" he asked calmly.

"He was weak." She narrowed her eyes.

Good God, had she murdered him? Gavin could see Peters, Yardley, and Ashbury sneaking up behind Mrs. Mulligan. He willed himself not to look at them and fix his attention on Mrs. Mulligan. He had to distract her.

"Mrs. Mulligan, I am none of these things you accuse me of." Margaux spoke, though her voice was still weak.

"Lies!" she hissed.

Beaujolais stepped next to Margaux to defend her, into Mrs. Mulligan's line of vision.

"You double before my eyes, God save our souls! Seize them!" she shouted to the crowd hysterically.

She had lifted one arm to point at the sisters with the sharp-pointed dibble, and Ashbury almost had Maili. Gavin shook his head at the Marquess. It was not worth risking.

The crowd was still standing around them, silent, listening to every word. Shock was written on every face.

"Let us go out and talk, shall we?" Gavin suggested again.

The woman narrowed her eyes, but followed through the doors Gavin opened.

Margaux felt some small relief at being out of the ballroom, though there was little breeze.

They were all now on the terrace, but Mrs. Mulligan was still holding on to Maili with a fierce grip. The little girl had stopped crying, but was clearly terrified. This could not go on indefinitely.

"Please let her go. Take me instead." Margaux pleaded.

Gavin squeezed her arm in warning. She ignored it and stepped forward to offer herself.

The crazed woman released Maili, who ran into Gavin's arms. Mrs. Mulligan lunged for Margaux, who held the dagger in her good hand. Margaux jumped back out of the way, desperately hoping it would not come to a scuffle between her and the woman. She came perilously close to the terrace edge and grabbed onto the ledge to steady herself. Margaux tried to calm her breathing, though all she could hear was the pounding of her heart in her ears. She waited for the woman's next move. The look in Mrs. Mulligan's eyes would forever haunt her—if she lived through this.

Mrs. Mulligan stumbled, but recovered and leapt toward her again, the sharp tool thrust directly at her. Margaux deflected the weapon with her bad hand, but her good hand with the dagger was pinned behind her against the ledge. She felt her strength weaken as she barely managed to shove the woman away. She saw her father and Gavin approaching from behind, but Mrs. Mulligan steadied herself and immediately charged at her again.

What happened next was a blur. Before anyone else could reach her, someone stepped in front of her and pushed Mrs. Mulligan over the railing. There was a scream and a horrible thudding sound.

When Margaux had the wherewithal to look over and see what had become of Mrs. Mulligan, Aunt Ida was standing beside Margaux with a satisfied gleam.

"*Vengeance is mine sayeth the Lord,*" Aunt Ida whispered.

CHAPTER 22

The ball had ended abruptly after Mrs. Mulligan's death. Margaux would ever be grateful that her mother had been there to take over her duties and see the guests on their way. She could not have smiled and said polite trivialities to anyone. It had been a relief to be ushered upstairs instead. Her mother's maid had whisked her out of her ball gown and brushed out her hair in a soothing ritual that almost made the evening seem commonplace.

She sat now in her room, in the armchair by the hearth, her knees pulled up to her chest, trembling and staring at the window. She had sent her mother and sister away, needing to be alone. The horrid final moments with Mrs. Mulligan played over and over in her mind. She had not realized Aunt Ida was even there. Apparently her aunt was there more often than anyone knew, thank heavens.

Margaux's reflection was not to last long. Maili was too scared to fall asleep, the nurse exclaimed in nervous tones when she came for Margaux.

She had been able to discover parts of the story from the nurse and Catriona, both wracked with guilt for not keeping better track of Maili.

As they made their way quickly to the nursery, Margaux was able to ascertain from the agitated nurse disjointed parts of what had happened. It seemed Mrs. Mulligan had drawn Maili away from the other children when she had been watching the dancing inside the ballroom. She'd told Maili her husband was hurt and needed Lord Craig, and so naturally Maili had wished to help. The footmen and guards posted near the door had gone to search for the girl as soon as she was discovered missing, and had not seen Mrs. Mulligan enter the ballroom with Maili.

When she saw the frightened child on entering the nursery, Margaux reflected she should have attended to Maili's comfort, rather than her own. Maili calmed instantly at the sight of her. Her fears had in all likelihood been for her new mama rather than herself.

Her trembling ceased, and with a few gentle strokes of her cheek and her hair, the girl fell asleep in Margaux's arms. The nurse and Catriona sought their own beds once Maili was finally resting. Gavin and her father were no doubt attending to the sordid details of dealing with the authorities and tidying up the mess. Margaux was grateful to be left out of that process. She selfishly wanted Gavin to be there with her, comforting her, as if they had a real marriage.

Her life had flashed before her eyes tonight, and she realized the only regret she would have had was her marriage. Oh, she was not regretting marrying Gavin. No. She was regretting the terms of the marriage. There were no clauses for falling in love.

Dawn was beginning to break over the horizon, she noticed. She wondered if Gavin had returned to his room, and she tried not to be resentful that he had not come to check on her. She needed no more than reassurance; there was nothing physically he could do for her. Nevertheless, she still coveted his embrace.

She must have dozed off to sleep when she felt his presence rather than heard it. Her eyelids were heavy and she struggled to open them.

"Shh, lass. I didna mean to wake you. I wasna expecting to find you here. I was looking in on the girls before coming down to you."

"Maili was upset," Margaux whispered in explanation.

Her eyes searched his as he knelt before her. He looked exhausted. He was stripped to his shirt-sleeves and breeches. His shirt was open at the neck and his hair was tousled. To her, he had never looked more handsome. She carefully disentangled herself from Maili, and Gavin scooped her into his arms the moment they were through the nursery door.

He deftly made his way down the nursery stairs and into her chamber, and gently placed her on the bed. She did not want to let go of him.

"Gavin," she whispered. The glow of a single taper flickered in his eyes, and all of her bold intentions flew out of the window. She needed him. She willed him to understand. She shyly touched his face. He seemed to comprehend her unspoken words. He buried his face in her hair and pulled her back into his arms.

"Margaux." He said her name as a caress.

"Please." She could not bring herself to ask. It seemed distasteful to ask one's husband to make theirs a true marriage, but she knew he would not do so unless she did. Her heart was lodged firmly in her throat, and she could not say the words.

He loosened his hold on her.

"I doona wanna take advantage of your shock."

"Please. I am ready to be your wife," She was reduced to begging. She had finally worked up the courage to give herself to him, and he insisted on being a gentleman.

"Margaux, I..." he hesitated.

Very well, she thought. He did not say he was opposed, and her mother's advice echoed in her mind. Perhaps he was trying to be a gentleman. She would never know unless she tried, and she might not find the courage again. She would show him what she could not find the words to say. She pulled back from him enough to find his face and she met his lips with her own. The sensation was dizzying and she trembled with longing.

"I do not know what to do," she confessed nervously.

"You are doing admirably thus far," he teased, but graciously proceeded to show her the way. It seemed her kind, gentle husband had repressed his passions and then unleashed them in that moment. He took her face between his hands and spoke to her with them and his lips, at first frenzied with desire, then soft and caressing.

"*Mo grádh,*" he whispered.

Words were no longer necessary, as they became lost in their embrace. They poured out their love for one another, and Margaux felt the peace and contentment she had longed for in their marriage.

~

Later that morning, as Margaux lay awake, trying to assimilate the change in her life and her marriage in the past few hours, it was almost too much to bear. She was never one to be swept away by emotion, but she felt she had earned a few tears over the past few weeks.

She felt an arm come about her, and a finger wiped away her tears.

"I suppose it too much to hope those are tears of joy?" Gavin asked gently in her ear.

She hiccupped a laugh. "I suppose some of them are."

His head was buried in her hair again and she felt him nod.

"Along with a few of gratefulness and humility." She inhaled a ragged, deep breath. "When I think about what could have happened..." She could not finish. He pulled her tightly to him, holding her as she sobbed.

"Doona think about it. You are here now. We will only think about the future."

"True. Everything we have been through has brought us to where we are now. Who knows where we would be if none of it had happened."

"I would like to think you would have succumbed to my charms anyhow and tossed out your silly terms," he teased.

"How was I to know you were perfect?" she reciprocated.

"I am not perfect, lass."

"I cannot think of a thing to support your claims."

"For one, I have been derelict in my duties as your doctor. Does it still hurt very much?"

He looked toward her bandages. He sat up and slowly began to remove them.

She shook her head and forced herself not to look away. She needed to see his face when he looked.

Instead of disgust, a look of tenderness swept over his face and bending his head over her arm, he began kissing his way from her hand to the top her cheek. He even kissed the twisted purple ropes and puckered scars that would always serve to remind her she wasn't perfect any more.

"I canna tell you how terrified I was last night," he said in a strained voice.

"I was as well," she said quietly.

"I doona ken how many more frights you can give me, wife. You have exceeded your rations for our entire marriage."

"I had best behave, then," she murmured mischievously.

"For many years to come," he agreed.

"I do not know what I did to deserve you, Gavin. I am afraid you have found yourself a bad bargain. I want to make it up to you."

"*Mo grádh*, we may not have married for love, but I have certainly found it. And I consider myself to be the luckiest lad on earth. Perhaps one day…"

It was her turn to shush him. She placed her fingers over his mouth.

"There is no one day. If I have learned anything from this dreadful experience, it is to live in the present. I have been afraid to show my love for you, to tell you how I felt; but no more."

"And I would never have forced you into anythin', but I confess to be verra, verra happy to reciprocate." He smiled devilishly and pulled her back into his embrace. Margaux felt like the most beautiful woman in the world.

When Margaux and Gavin found they were able to face the world, which was perhaps prompted solely by the need to check on the children, they made their way to join the others around the breakfast table. Gavin saw Margaux blush as she met the knowing faces of her family, while he was greeted with congratulatory winks and nods.

One would scarce credit the events of the past night from the jovial cheer of the household that morn.

"How are you, *chérie?*" Lady Ashbury greeted her daughter.

"I confess I am a bit tired," Margaux said, and then blushed again. He suspected she was worried they knew of her and Gavin's night-time activities.

"That is understandable, my dear," Lord Ashbury remarked. He turned to Gavin. "We found the vicar, earlier this morning, behind the gardener's shed. It seems he came to his senses and tried to stop Mrs. Mulligan, and was clubbed over the head for his insolence."

"He is still alive?" Gavin asked, ever the doctor.

"Aye, he was taken to the nearest cottage by Buchanan. He did not think it right to have Mulligan near the house. Mulligan will keep for now."

"You saw him?" Gavin asked with surprise.

Lord Ashbury nodded as he sipped his coffee.

"I will deal with him after breakfast," Gavin said, unsure how he felt about the information. He looked toward his wife, who had paled at the news. He reached out to take her hand. She looked up and smiled at him. His heart began to race at the love he saw in her look.

"I wonder if we will ever be able to make sense of it all," Margaux wondered aloud.

"Sometimes it is best not to know," Gavin said softly, rubbing his thumb soothingly over the back of her hand.

"Mulligan was muttering quite a bit," Lord Ashbury confessed. "He was trying to excuse his wife's delirium."

"Excuse it?" Margaux asked, incredulity in her tone.

"It seems both she and Mrs. Bailey had been taken advantage of as girls," Lord Ashbury began.

"Then why…" Margaux looked stupefied.

"I did not get a full, coherent account, mind you, but it seems Mrs. Bailey felt called to help the poor girls, whereas Mrs. Mulligan was brought to believe the abuse had been asked for—that it was her fault," he explained.

"And she made it her mission to rid the village of the filth," Gavin added distastefully.

"I had wondered why Mrs. Bailey was in the main house that night," Margaux said.

"It appears she was there trying to warn you, or save you," Jolie replied.

"Poor woman," Lady Ashbury said sadly.

"One of the girls recalled seeing Mrs. Bailey arguing with a lady on the night of the fire, before she went missing and I found her in the house. The girl also mentioned Mrs. Bailey telling the woman she wasn't supposed to be there, so maybe Mrs. Mulligan thought her sister would not be burned," Gavin reasoned aloud.

"Only the harlots," Margaux retorted.

"It does explain why she set fire to the house her sister lived in," Ashbury replied.

"I wonder if that is why Mrs. Bailey tried to keep me from helping at the Dower House." Margaux voiced her thoughts, obviously attempting to make sense of the madness.

"Perhaps, but we will likely never know the whole story," Gavin reflected, still holding her hand. "It seems a troubled soul is at rest. All we can do is attempt to help the vicar."

"As long as he won't preach here again," Margaux said with a guilty smile.

"He can preach as much as he likes from his cell in the gaol. He may not have instigated the murders, but he did not stop them. I have little doubt, when the vicar is questioned, we will find my brother's death was no accident."

This statement was met with murmurs and gasps of surprise.

"I do not doubt them capable, but what makes you suspicious?" Ashbury asked.

"When I went back over everything in my head, it completed the puzzle. There were many pieces that alone were innocent. For instance, Lady Ida mentioned she thought they would be gone by now, which I now understand to mean the Mulligans. But until I heard Ashbury tell me Iain had meant to replace the vicar and died before that happened, I wasn't certain the deaths were not accidental."

"Then there was the fire that caused Iain to move his journals to the dungeon," Margaux added.

"Aye. And the family had ceased to attend church, but Wallace didna ken the vicar had been dismissed, since he had retired. He only came back to help after I arrived. If I had ken Iain had dismissed them, I woulda taken her threats more seriously."

"Do you think the wheels were sabotaged? The day we went into the village..." Margaux's voice trailed off in remembrance.

"I do. I think that was the final piece of the puzzle for me. I am thankful no one else was hurt. When a lunatic snaps, no one is safe. As we saw, Mrs. Mulligan had transferred her obsession to Margaux. Either way, I will never have my brother back, but I suppose it brings a small measure of resolution."

The family took their leave after breakfast, and Gavin and Margaux sat in the garden, looking out over the loch, enjoying their first moment of peace together since their marriage. It was another warm, sunny morning, and the scent of lilacs, roses, and peonies intoxicated Margaux's senses as bees buzzed around doing their work. She felt she had been sent to heaven overnight, such was the change in circumstance during the past four-and-twenty hours.

"Gavin?" she asked.

"Yes, *mo grádh?*" he said tenderly.

"I have wanted to ask you what you said to me in Gaelic at our wedding," she confessed.

"*Tugaim mo chroí duit go deo?*" He looked down at her with so much love in his eyes as he stroked her cheek, Margaux could only wonder she had not realized before.

"Yes. It has been on my mind constantly," she whispered.

"I give you my heart forever," he said, before leaning down to her and kissing her in a way that left no doubt at all.

"How could you say so, then? When you only married me for convenience?" she asked, when she had recovered.

"*Mo grádh*, my love," he translated. "I gave you my heart knowing that love would follow. I think I realized long before you did."

"I am not certain when I knew," she wondered aloud.

"It matters not when, only that you do." He smiled at her, and her heart felt as if it would overflow.

"Yes. I can only be grateful that some greater power knew more than we did and took a hand in bringing us together," she reflected.

"Even through fire."

PREVIEW OF MELTING THE ICE

*W*hat man wants to marry unless he needs an heir?" Benedict asked scathingly.

"There are those who find companionship, if not love with a lady, Your Grace," Hughes remarked encouragingly, with little regard for His Grace's tone.

"Ladies are good for one thing only," Benedict retorted.

"But you must marry one of them to produce a legitimate heir."

"Must I?" he asked softly with an underlying challenge in his voice.

"The last heir has died, Your Grace."

"You are certain?" he asked rhetorically.

"Quite, quite certain. Mr. Norton has made an exhaustive search." The secretary held up the damning news just received from the solicitor.

"I see."

"It must be done, Your Grace."

Benedict Stanton, Duke of Yardley, sighed loudly. He was now faced with the one thing he'd vowed never to do again: marry. He remained silent, digesting this new-found information along with his beefsteak and kidney pie, which was suddenly souring his stomach.

The duke's secretary was used to His Grace's ways, and stood quietly while his employer made a decision.

Benedict exhaled audibly again.

"I suppose, Hughes, that you have made me a list?"

"Yes, Your Grace." The ever efficient secretary promptly produced a list with twelve names and their resumes, including bloodlines, properties, and dowries.

"As you can see, Your Grace, I have listed them in order of eligibility." He paused.

Benedict shooed the list away.

"You may begin negotiations with the first one on the list. I have little care for their qualities other than breeding."

The secretary cleared his throat nervously, which produced an elevated eyebrow from His Grace.

"I also took the liberty of providing those considered to be the Incomparables."

The secretary placed the list on the desk before the duke.

"Incomparable is synonymous with idiot, Hughes. Is there a point?"

"Perhaps not quite synonymous, Your Grace. Let me tactfully say that some of the eligibles are not necessarily of prime stock, whereas others..." he said leadingly, using horseflesh terminology most like to convince the duke who preferred equine company to human.

"I care little for appearances," the Duke retorted.

"I think it best for you to make the decision, Your Grace. Or I could ask the Duchess..."

His Grace ignored the last taunt about involving his mother. "I should send you to negotiations with," he glanced at the first name on the list, "Cohen's daughter, a Lady Mary, but I gather you do not approve?"

"Lady Mary is all that is amiable, Your Grace, but she resembles your finest Arabians and she titters."

The Duke cringed. Perhaps a mite of scrutiny would be called for.

"Have you seen all of them?"

The secretary flushed red. "Certainly, Your Grace."

Yardley stared in stupefaction at his normally staid secretary blushing like a fresh youth.

"Very well. Make an offer to the first one you deem most suitable to my preferences."

The secretary bowed and left the room.

Benedict wanted little to do with any female ever again, unless they had four legs. It had been nearly ten years since his first fiasco of a marriage, and the taste in his mouth was as bitter as the day it had happened.

Jolie pulled her horse to a halt as she skirted the edge of the chalk cliffs, inhaling the scent of the sea. As fond as she was of London, the reprieve to her cousin, Lord Easton's, house in Sussex had been welcome. This Season did not boast any new suitors she could take seriously, and her family had all departed England, leaving her feeling lonely for the first time that she could remember.

She would return to London soon with Lady Easton as her chaperone, but there was no one serious contender for her affections. She would never confess to anyone, save her sisters, her fears of becoming a spinster. Her sister, Margaux, would rather that than marry someone she could not love. But not Jolie. She wished for a good match with someone she could respect, and who could make her life comfortable. She was not so mercenary as to accept anyone. She had, in fact, turned down so many proposals she had been teasingly nicknamed Ice, though nothing could be less apt to describe her. She had simply never found said qualities in one person. She did not require a title, contrary to popular belief. But being a duchess certainly would not hurt, she thought mockingly to herself.

She urged her horse onwards again, and enjoyed an exhilarating gallop across the downs while the wind whipped at her with all its might. Her cousin had famous breeding stables, and she was enjoying the fruits of them immensely. Riding—no, galloping—was the one thing she missed the most when in town.

As she entered the house, stripping off her riding gloves and handing her crop to the butler, she was informed that her father's man of business awaited her company in the library.

"Thank you, Barnes." She smiled charmingly at the elderly earl's butler who had served her uncle Wyndham since before she was born. Why would her father's solicitor be seeking her out? It was Anjou who was awaiting news. Perhaps there was news of Aidan, and just after Anjou had set out! She tidied her wind-blown hair as much as she could and she entered the doorway to find her cousin, Mr. Harlow, and another man in deep conversation. She paused and knocked.

"Ah, Jolie. Please join us," Lord Easton said as all of the men stood.

"Lady Beaujolais, may I present Mr. Norton, and you are acquainted with Mr. Harlow, I believe."

She nodded as the men bowed. She took her seat curiously and looked to her cousin.

"Jolie, Mr. Norton is here on behalf of the Duke of Yardley."

What has that to do with me? She wondered, but kept her tongue. Her pulse sped up nevertheless. She had heard of Yardley, the duke who was reputed to be cold and reclusive, but had never met him herself.

"I will let you explain, Mr. Norton if you would," her cousin said.

"Your ladyship, I will be brief. His Grace has decided to marry, and has selected you as his choice."

An unaccountable wave of anger swept through her. Was the duke sending his proposal of marriage through his solicitor without so much as an introduction? How dared he! He felt himself to be above common civilities? True, it was flattering in some respects, but she would never marry someone so arrogant, so...so...she could not even think of a proper word to describe the audacity! Had he made an arrangement with her father to pay his addresses? No, her father would never. She sat in silence attempting to control her temper and manage a dignified response. All that came from her mouth was, "I see."

The solicitor interpreted her silence as shocked pleasure, and continued. "He has made you a most generous settlement, my lady."

He handed her a piece of paper outlining his offer. She struggled to keep the paper from shaking in her hands.

"You will be settled in high style, with your own house and estate and several thousand pounds a year. And it is not contingent on providing an heir," the solicitor said, as if she should be flattered.

Jolie could feel her cousin's eyes on her. She met them with her own questioningly, and could see by his expression that he was as shocked as she was. How would her father have handled this? She supposed Easton felt it was her decision to make. Jolie had to take a deep breath so she did not strangle the messenger. She stood and waved the men back to their seats while she walked to the window, her thoughts in a whirl.

After a few moments she turned and asked, "Sir, would you be so good as to inform His Grace that I would rather rot in hell than accept his offer."

She tore the settlement in two and dropped it in his lap.

"Gentlemen," she said as she walked out of the room.

OTHER TITLES BY ELIZABETH JOHNS:

ABOUT THE AUTHOR

Like many writers, Elizabeth Johns was first an avid reader, though she was a reluctant convert. It was Jane Austen's clever wit and unique turn of phrase that hooked Johns when she was 'forced' to read Pride and Prejudice for a school assignment. She began writing when she ran out of her favourite author's books and decided to try her hand at crafting a Regency romance novel. Her journey into publishing began with the release of Surrender the Past, book one of the Loring-Abbott Series. Johns makes no pretensions to Austen's wit, but hopes readers will perhaps laugh and find some enjoyment in her writing.

Johns attributes much of her inspiration to her mother, a former English teacher. During their last summer together, Johns would sit on the porch swing and read her stories to her mother, who encouraged her to continue writing. Busy with multiple careers, including a professional job in the medical field, writing, and mother of small children, Johns squeezes in time for reading whenever possible.

PREVIEW OF MELTING THE ICE

*W*hat man wants to marry unless he needs an heir?" Benedict asked scathingly.

"There are those who find companionship, if not love with a lady, your Grace," Hughes remarked encouragingly, with little regard for His Grace's tone.

"Ladies are good for one thing only," Benedict retorted.

"But you must marry one of them to produce a legitimate heir."

"Must I?" he asked softly with an underlying challenge in his voice.

"The last heir has died, your Grace."

"You are certain?" he asked rhetorically.

"Quite, quite certain. Mr. Norton has made an exhaustive search." The secretary held up the damning news just received from the solicitor.

"I see."

"It must be done, your Grace."

Benedict Stanton, Duke of Yardley, sighed loudly. He was now faced with the one thing he'd vowed never to do again: marry. He remained silent, digesting this new-found information along with his beefsteak and kidney pie, which was suddenly souring his stomach.

The duke's secretary was used to His Grace's ways, and stood quietly while his employer made a decision.

Benedict exhaled audibly again.

"I suppose, Hughes, that you have made me a list?"

"Yes, your Grace." The ever efficient secretary promptly produced a list with twelve names and their resumes, including bloodlines, properties, and dowries.

"As you can see, your Grace, I have listed them in order of eligibility." He paused.

Benedict shooed the list away.

"You may begin negotiations with the first one on the list. I have little care for their qualities other than breeding."

The secretary cleared his throat nervously, which produced an elevated eyebrow from His Grace.

"I also took the liberty of providing those considered to be the Incomparables."

The secretary placed the list on the desk before the duke.

"Incomparable is synonymous with idiot, Hughes. Is there a point?"

"Perhaps not quite synonymous, your Grace. Let me tactfully say that some of the eligibles are not necessarily of prime stock, whereas others..." he said leadingly, using horseflesh terminology most like to convince the duke who preferred equine company to human.

"I care little for appearances," the Duke retorted.

"I think it best for you to make the decision, your Grace. Or I could ask the Duchess..."

His Grace ignored the last taunt about involving his mother. "I should send you to negotiations with," he glanced at the first name on the list, "Cohen's daughter, a Lady Mary, but I gather you do not approve?"

"Lady Mary is all that is amiable, your Grace, but she resembles your finest Arabians and she titters."

The Duke cringed. Perhaps a mite of scrutiny would be called for.

"Have you seen all of them?"

The secretary flushed red. "Certainly, your Grace."

Yardley stared in stupefaction at his normally staid secretary blushing like a fresh youth.

"Very well. Make an offer to the first one you deem most suitable to my preferences."

The secretary bowed and left the room.

Benedict wanted little to do with any female ever again, unless they had four legs. It had been nearly ten years since his first fiasco of a marriage, and the taste in his mouth was as bitter as the day it had happened.

Jolie pulled her horse to a halt as she skirted the edge of the chalk cliffs, inhaling the scent of the sea. As fond as she was of London, the reprieve to her cousin, Lord Easton's, house in Sussex had been welcome. This Season did not boast any new suitors she could take seriously, and her family had all departed England, leaving her feeling lonely for the first time that she could remember.

She would return to London soon with Lady Easton as her chaperone, but there was no one serious contender for her affections. She would never confess to anyone, save her sisters, her fears of becoming a spinster. Her sister, Margaux, would rather that than marry someone she could not love. But not Jolie. She wished for a good match with someone she could respect, and who could make her life comfortable. She was not so mercenary as to accept anyone. She had, in fact, turned down so many proposals she had been teasingly nicknamed Ice, though nothing could be less apt to describe her. She had simply never found said qualities in one person. She did not require a title, contrary to popular belief. But being a duchess certainly would not hurt, she thought mockingly to herself.

She urged her horse onwards again, and enjoyed an exhilarating gallop across the downs while the wind whipped at her with all its might. Her cousin had famous breeding stables, and she was enjoying the fruits of them immensely. Riding—no, galloping—was the one thing she missed the most when in town.

As she entered the house, stripping off her riding gloves and handing her crop to the butler, she was informed that her father's man of business awaited her company in the library.

"Thank you, Barnes." She smiled charmingly at the elderly earl's butler who had served her uncle Wyndham since before she was born. Why would her father's solicitor be seeking her out? It was Anjou who was awaiting news. Perhaps there was news of Aidan, and just after Anjou had set out! She tidied her wind-blown hair as much as she could and she entered the doorway to find her cousin, Mr. Harlow, and another man in deep conversation. She paused and knocked.

"Ah, Jolie. Please join us," Lord Easton said as all of the men stood.

"Lady Beaujolais, may I present Mr. Norton, and you are acquainted with Mr. Harlow, I believe."

She nodded as the men bowed. She took her seat curiously and looked to her cousin.

"Jolie, Mr. Norton is here on behalf of the Duke of Yardley."

What has that to do with me? She wondered, but kept her tongue. Her pulse sped up nevertheless. She had heard of Yardley, the duke who was reputed to be cold and reclusive, but had never met him herself.

"I will let you explain, Mr. Norton if you would," her cousin said.

"Your ladyship, I will be brief. His Grace has decided to marry, and has selected you as his choice."

An unaccountable wave of anger swept through her. Was the duke sending his proposal of marriage through his solicitor without so much as an introduction? How dared he! He felt himself to be above common civilities? True, it was flattering in some respects, but she would never marry someone so arrogant, so...so...she could not even think of a proper word to describe the audacity! Had he made an arrangement with her father to pay his addresses? No, her father would never. She sat in silence attempting to control her temper and manage a dignified response. All that came from her mouth was, "I see."

The solicitor interpreted her silence as shocked pleasure, and continued. "He has made you a most generous settlement, my lady."

He handed her a piece of paper outlining his offer. She struggled to keep the paper from shaking in her hands.

"You will be settled in high style, with your own house and estate and several thousand pounds a year. And it is not contingent on providing an heir," the solicitor said, as if she should be flattered.

Jolie could feel her cousin's eyes on her. She met them with her own questioningly, and could see by his expression that he was as shocked as she was. How would her father have handled this? She supposed Easton felt it was her decision to make. Jolie had to take a deep breath so she did not strangle the messenger. She stood and waved the men back to their seats while she walked to the window, her thoughts in a whirl.

After a few moments she turned and asked, "Sir, would you be so good as to inform His Grace that I would rather rot in hell than accept his offer."

She tore the settlement in two and dropped it in his lap.

"Gentlemen," she said as she walked out of the room.

AFTERWORD

Author's note: British spellings and grammar have been used in an effort to reflect what would have been done in the time period in which the novels are set. While I realize all words may not be exact, I hope you can appreciate the differences and effort made to be historically accurate while attempting to retain readability for the modern audience.

Thank you for reading *Through the Fire*. I hope you enjoyed it. If you did, please help other readers find this book:

1. This ebook is lendable, so send it to a friend who you think might like it so she or he can discover me, too.

2. Help other people find this book by writing a review.

3. Sign up for my new releases at www.Elizabethjohnsauthor.com, so you can find out about the next book as soon as it's available.

4. Come like my Facebook page www.facebook.com/ Elizabethjohnsauthor or follow on Twitter @Ejohnsauthor or write me at elizabethjohnsauthor@gmail.com

Made in the USA
Las Vegas, NV
05 April 2022